Bastards and Angels

Draconic Crimson MC

Book 2, the Sinners Series

K. Renee

Theresa,
every bastard
needs an
angel to
save him.

♡ KRenee

Content

Copyright

Dedication

Chapter One

Chapter Two

Chapter Three

Chapter Four

Chapter Five

Chapter Six

Chapter Seven

Chapter Eight

Chapter Nine

Chapter Ten

Chapter Eleven

Chapter Twelve

Chapter Thirteen

Chapter Fourteen

Chapter Fifteen

Chapter Sixteen

Chapter Seventeen

Chapter Eighteen

Chapter Nineteen

Chapter Twenty

Chapter Twenty-One

Chapter Twenty-Two

Chapter Twenty-Three

Chapter Twenty-Four

Chapter Twenty-Five

Chapter Twenty-Six

About the Author

Acknowledgments

Copyright

Bastards and Angels

© 2016 K. Renee

Published by K. Renee

1st Edition

All rights reserved. No part of this book may be reproduced or transmitted in any form, including electronic or mechanical, without written permission from the publisher, except in the case of brief quotations embodied in critical articles or reviews.

This is a work of fiction. Names, characters, businesses, places, events, and incidents are either the products of the author's imagination or used in a fictitious manner. Any resemblance to actual persons, living or dead, or actual events is purely coincidental.

This book is licensed for your personal enjoyment only. It may not be re-sold or given away to others. If you would like to share this book, please purchase an additional copy for each person. If you are reading this book and did not purchase it, or it was not purchased for your use only, you should return it to the seller and purchase your own copy. Thank you for respecting the author's work.

Published: K. Renee - 2016

k.renee.author@gmail.com

Cover Design: KLa Boutique - Swag

https://www.facebook.com/pages/KLa-Boutique-Swag/908193265872628

Formatting: K. Renee

Cover Photo: © Wander Aguiar

https://www.facebook.com/Wander-Book-Club-461833027360302

Cover Model: Marshall Perrin

https://www.facebook.com/Marshall-Perrin-353122568171465/

Editor: TCB Editing Services

https://www.facebook.com/TCBEditing/?fref=ts

ISBN-13: 978-1537155128

ISBN-10: 1537155121

So you can drag me through Hell
If it meant I could hold your hand
-BMTH

Prologue

Six Hours. Five Minutes. Sixteen Seconds.

That is all it took for one woman to grab a hold on me. Her fiery spirit and smokin' hot legs drive me fuckin' crazy. She has no clue what I would do for her, but I finally get why Stavros is such a pussy when it comes to Harlyn.

I knew that shit wouldn't be easy with her and, even though I wanted nothing more than to own that red head, I jumped in dick first and didn't think about the consequences. Every kiss, touch and suck from her mouth took me from the loveless marriage I've been tied to for way too fuckin' long. I never thought that I would ever end up leaving that bitch, Tina, but the more I think about Trix and my son, the more I want to get the fuck away from her so I can be the father and man that I'm supposed to be.

At first, I didn't want to admit that I was his father. But, after all the shit that I watched Stavros go through, I don't want to lose him or his mother because I'm a coward.

Now that the lock down is over, Tina's stupid ass is at the house again and I've been spending my nights in the fuckin' clubhouse. I fucked Trix all through her pregnancy, even when I didn't believe Blade was mine. The only thing that put the brakes on us is being at the clubhouse with my wife. Shit, I'd never met him until she showed up with him on her hip.

Just thinking about the last time I had that girl under me turns me on. Before I can even reach for my phone to call her, there is a soft knock on the door. Getting up from my bed, I adjust myself and swing it open. Her tear-streaked face is the first thing that catches my attention. I don't see our son anywhere in sight, so I pull her into my room.

"E," she whispers. I hook an arm around her,

and pull her body to mine. She sobs against my chest for a few minutes before I grab her chin and force her to look at me.

"What's wrong?" My whole body tenses with worry and, when she doesn't say anything, I ask about Blade. "Is Blade okay?"

She wipes at her tears, but it doesn't stop her from crying. I walk us over to the bed and take a seat, pulling her into my lap. "Baby, I need you to tell me what's wrong." She hiccups and wipes her nose with her hand. "I can't do anything if I don't know what you need from me."

"I had a visit from CPS. Apparently, someone called them and told them that I was abusing Blade." I feel anger course through my veins and I reach over for my phone. I swear to God if that bitch did this, I'll slit her damn throat.

"What are you doing?" she asks, wide eyed. I search for that bitch's contact and hit the number when it appears. When she answers, I don't bother being fuckin' nice. I could care less if I hurt her damn feelings. She's crossed the damn line, and I won't hesitate to making her pay.

"Hello, E. Are you finally coming home to satisfy your wife?" I feel Trix tense in my arms when she hears the bitch.

"No, I fuckin' called because you are fuckin' with the wrong person. Call off your fuckin' dogs, and stay the fuck away from Trixie and my son. You make another call to CPS, and I won't give you a warning next time." I seethe. She wants to play fuckin' games? I'll show her just how much far I'll take it.

"I don't know what you're talking about, E. I didn't call anyone. But maybe that whore isn't so fit to raise your son." I can hear the venom in her tone and, if I were in the same room as her, I'd fuckin' kill her.

"No, cunt you aren't fit to raise that boy. Call it off or I'll make you wish you never met me." I hang up before she can even say anything else. Looking down at Trix, I see her hands clenched into fists and the tears silently running down her face.

"Why would she do something that hateful?" She and I both know the answer to that, but I don't say anything. I don't even know what to say. That bitch isn't the same woman I married right out of high school. I should have fuckin' listened when all my buddies told me that she was a snake in sheep's clothing. But, like a fuckin' idiot, I was only thinking with my dick. She fucked like a porn star, and sucked my dick better than any bitch I'd ever known. Well… until now.

"She wants what you have. She is jealous that you had my son, and all she fuckin' has from me is a ring." I move the red hair from her face and tuck it behind her ear. "I won't let them take him away from you." I press my lips against her forehead. Her fingers dig into my back, and the only thing I can think of is making sure that her and Blade are always taken care of.

"E." She whispers. Her small hand cups my cheek, and I know that she's about to say something that I'm going to fuckin' hate. It's what she always does when things get rough. When she told me she was pregnant, I flipped the fuck out. She put her hand on my cheek just like she's doing now and, after she delivered the news, I put a hole in the wall before I left the fuckin' clubhouse.

I drove for days after her news, and I didn't even bother to call her when I got back. I threw all my time and energy into working on my bike and working out with Stavros. At first, I didn't even bother thinking about her until I couldn't help myself and every thought of mine focused on her again. Of course, it didn't take long before we started fuckin' again.

"Just fuckin' spit it out, Trix. I'm a grown man. I can handle it." A frown mars her perfect face, and I hate that I'm being a dick to her. She deserves so much more than me and this shit that I seem to drag into her life.

"I can't keep up with this shit. She is slowly ruining my life and…" She trails off and I want to tell her that I'll be done with her, but I don't know if I can. I tried when I figured out that I was in love with Trix, but Tina threatened to kill herself. Maybe I should have let her, and then I wouldn't be getting this speech from Trix right fuckin' now. "I'm afraid for Blade's safety. Maybe…" She looks down at her hands that are twisting together.

She doesn't want to do it just as much as I don't want to hear her say the words. "We should just end it for good." A tear slides down her cheek, and I can't help but focus on it. I don't want to see the pain in her eyes, and I don't want to listen to her damn words. We've ended this thing between us more times than I can count, but we always come back for more. She pulls me in and wraps her arms around my heart, even when I fuckin' want nothing to do with her. Right now, I don't want to let go.

"Elec, please say something," she pleads when I don't say anything for a long time.

"What do you want me to say?" I bark out. She shrinks back and a tear trails down her face. She doesn't want me to say what I am really thinking right now. It will only push her further away from me, and I don't want to do that.

"I just…" She bites her bottom lip, and I wish it were me doing it. My spine is so ramrod straight with anger and hurt that I can't move. "I want you to be part of his life, but…" She doesn't finish her sentence. I already know what she's going to say. She doesn't want my wife anywhere near him. Tina has already fucked things up between Trix and me, and is only trying to make Trix pay for being the other woman.

"You don't want him near Tina. Yeah, I get that. She won't go near him. You have my word." She nods her head slowly, and her eyes never leave the ground. "You need money? You come to me, not my Prez. He's not the one that knocked you up, so he doesn't need to help you. Blade is mine, and I won't let either of you want for anything." Her eyes meet mine and they widen a fraction.

"How…?" She didn't think he'd tell me.

"Prez told me what he did. I told him to take it out of my cut. I won't let another man raise my son, or pay for the things he needs. I'm his father, and I'll be the only father he knows." Her eyes finally meet mine and I see anger in them.

"You have no say in that anymore," she sneers. "You made that choice when you promised me a forever, and all I ever got was lies. You said you were leaving her, and now she's trying to get my son taken away from me. You didn't even believe that he was yours. I did it all by myself, and look what it's gotten me!" She yells at me.

She turns to walk towards the door and I reach out, grabbing her arm. "Don't," she whispers. Her anger is gone, and it's replaced with the hurt and sadness that I always seem to bring her. "Just let me go, E. I don't want to fight with you anymore, and I sure as hell don't want to be your second choice. Blade and I deserve more. We deserve the happily ever after."

She pulls out of my grip, and I watch her walk towards the door. She doesn't even bother turning around one last time. Her head tilts towards the ground before I see her shoulders heave and she walks out the door. Watching the door that she walked through, I can feel my heart break into a million different pieces. She needs to know that I would never let Tina take Blade away from her. Grabbing my phone from my pocket, I dial Prez's number and wait for him to answer. He's been on edge all damn week since he got out of the hospital, but I don't know what else to do.

"Yeah, E?" He answers on the third ring. He sounds pissed off and, even though I don't want to add to it, I need to protect Trix and Blade from my wife.

"Tina called CPS on Trix. She's trying to get my son taken away from his mother." I hear him say fuck a couple of times before he sighs and tells me to come to his office. "I'll be there in a minute," I answer before hitting the END button.

Making my way to his office, I stop and stare at the door for a minute before I knock. I need to get rid of that bitch. She's fuckin' slowly draining the damn life out of me, and I don't want to lose the only good fuckin' thing in my life because I couldn't cut the fuckin' cord when I know it is the right thing.

Knocking, I hear him yell out for me to come in. When I open the door, I see the bottle of Johnny sitting on his desk, and he's leaning back in his chair, nursing a glass of the liquor. "Take a seat," he mutters. I shut the door and take a seat across from the man I've looked up to since I joined this club. He doesn't always seem to have his head on straight, but he protects what's his and never backs down from a fight.

"What happened?" he asks. He doesn't ever sugarcoat shit, and I'm grateful for that.

"Tina called CPS, and now Trix wants nothing to do with me." He snorts at that, and I tighten my hands into fists in my lap.

"Finally, she's getting smart. I told Trix to stay the fuck away from you from day one, but you charmed the panties off of her and put her under your goddamn spell." I shake my head at him and watch him.

"I fuckin' love her," I state when he doesn't say anything else.

"Then it doesn't sound like it's a hard decision. " He deadpans like I'm an idiot and shouldn't need advice from him. "Call the CPS fuckers, and tell them that your wife is a vindictive bitch who is trying to get your son taken from his mom because she's a jealous bitch. I don't know what else to tell you, kid. You want Trix, fight for her. Don't let her walk away so easily because, if you do, someone else is going to take your place."

I feel anger coarse through my veins at that last statement. My VP has been sniffing around her for fuckin' weeks. Ever since the lock down, he's been going out of his way to help her out. "You mean Romeo," I grit out.

He chuckles at my tone, and I don't feel like its fuckin' funny one bit. He isn't taking my girl. I don't give a fuck who he is. "Then I suggest you don't give him any more opportunities than you already have." I nod and stand from my chair. I'll make her listen to me if it's the last thing I do. She doesn't get to walk away from this shit just because she thinks I'm not all in. I am, and I'll make sure she stays the fuck away from my VP.

My mind wanders back to the lockdown, and having both Trix and Tina in the same place for a period of time.

"Does she know?" Stavros asks.

"That I sneak in here? No, she'd be pissed. I fucked

this shit up so damn bad. I want to be part of his life." I run my hands over my face and I get it. I'm fuckin' pissed that I didn't believe Trix. I should have just listened to her when she told me he was mine. I wouldn't be missing out on his damn life like I am. "Tina is starting to put it together. I can only imagine what she's going to say when she sees him closer up. Trix has stayed as far away from us as she can since she got here, not that I blame her."

"Why aren't you giving her money?" Stavros doesn't flip the fuck out like I thought he would. He loves them like they are his family. I don't blame him. I love her, too, even if I'm too stupid to tell her.

I close my eyes and shake my head. "For the longest time, I didn't want to believe that he was mine. Trix sleeps with all the brothers." He cuts me off, but I don't blame him. He probably thinks I'm goin' to bad mouth her.

"She hasn't slept with any of the brothers in the last year. I told her it was her choice when she came to me. She wanted out of the game, and I gave her a job working at one of the clubs as a waitress. That way, she was making money and being able to provide for herself." I can feel the shock

register on my face. I had no fuckin' clue. Hell, I don't even want to believe it now. There is no fuckin' way she only came here for me.

"She only came around for me?" He shrugs his shoulders, but doesn't really give me a straight answer.

"I only know that she wanted to make a change in her life and I gave her the opportunity. I could tell she was in love with someone. I just didn't know who until she showed up pregnant and alone. You broke her when you said you didn't want anything to do with her after she got pregnant. Probably because you thought you weren't the father, but brother there is no denying that little boy is yours." I nod, but don't say anything.

"Yet you still called her when you wanted your dick sucked or a fuck. She isn't your damn plaything. You will be providing for Blade. I don't give a fuck what happens in your marriage because of this. Man the fuck up, and take care of your kid."

I nod in agreement, because I will *take care of my boy. There is no doubt that I will. He's mine, and I'm claiming him. "I will Prez."*

"I gave her money the other day. She's working her ass off, and doesn't have a pot to piss in." My Prez giving her money pisses me off. It should be me that takes care of them. He should know that there is no way that I'll just let him give her money.

"Take what you gave her out of my cut. Every time. I want to take care of them." Prez nods his head and, when we look over to the bed, Blade is awake and reaching out for Stavros. Part of me wishes that it was me he wanted, but he doesn't know me at all.

A little hand reaches out towards me, and I don't know what to do. Stavros moves closer towards me, and I reach out to grab Blade's chubby little hand. Blade looks up at me and watches my every move. I feel the emotions take over me, and I don't know how to handle the feelings that are running through me. The door flies open, and I watch as Tina comes barging in. Fuck. This is all I fuckin' need. That bitch better not say one word about Trix or Blade. "You're fuckin' that whore, aren't you? Where is she?" Tina starts looking around the room for Trix, but I walk over to her and grab her waist, pulling her towards the door and away from my son.

"Shut the fuck up," I growl when I push her into the wall behind her. She tries to fight me. She's no match for me, and I can see the anger build up inside of her until the baby starts to cry. She instantly stops struggling against me and her eyes move to him.

"You son of a bitch," she hisses. She tries to get out of my grip to get closer to Stavros and Blade, but I never let her ass go. I pull her bitch ass out of the room and push her against the wall. Stavros takes Blade towards the kitchen to his mom.

"I fucking hate you, you lying bastard. What does that bitch have that I don't?" she screams at me.

"Fuckin' class, you stupid cunt. Stay the fuck away from both of them." I growl in her ear. I hear their footsteps coming towards us and it only makes Tina fight harder against me.

When they get close enough to us, Tina turns her anger onto Trix. She points at Trix and starts screaming at her. "You stupid slut. I will make sure you regret ever touching my old man. That kid is never going to know his father. I'll make sure of it."

Trix doesn't let the words affect her, and I have to admire that. She's a strong woman, and that's one of the things I love about her. "Get your fuckin' ol' lady on a leash, E. I won't have that type of disrespect in front of a child," Stavros demands. Tina shrinks back at Stavros's words, partly because she's afraid of him. When he makes a threat, it isn't for show. It's a damn promise if you cross him.

When I finally get her ass out of the hallway, I push her into my room and shut the door behind us. "You ever go anywhere near either of them, I will fuckin' kill you. Stay the fuck away from Trix and my son." She slightly nods her head, and I walk away and back through the door, slamming it on my way out.

Chapter One

After meeting with Prez, I make my way into the clubhouse to see Trix talking to Romeo. Almost like he can feel my eyes burning into him, he looks up and gives me a grin. We've already almost come to blows over her before, and there isn't anything that will keep me from going after the bastard if he makes his move on her.

He puts his hand on her shoulder, almost like he's comforting her. She looks up to him and sees that he's looking behind her. When she turns around, she sees me watching them. Her eyes meet mine, and she takes a step closer to him. Her hand reaches out to touch him and I see red. I don't even give a fuck if this gets me in trouble with the club. He has his hands on my girl.

Stalking my way towards them, I grab her wrist and pull her behind my body. Her startled gasp doesn't stop me from getting in his face. The whole room goes silent, and I can feel everyone's eyes on us. "Stay the fuck away from her," I growl. Romeo smirks at me, and I feel her put her hands on my back.

"You don't own me, E!" she yells at my back. I don't even bother with what she says; she's wrong. I do own her, and I won't let anyone else take what's mine.

Turning to face her, I grab her chin and force her to look at me. "I do own you. He touches you, and I'll make sure you never see our son again." She gasps at my threat, and I release her chin. Her eyes meet Romeo's and I turn to face him. "You want her to lose her son? Then, keep trying to get into her panties. Go for my sloppy seconds." I watch his expression change from calm to pissed in a matter of seconds. There isn't a whole lot that pisses my VP off, but this does.

He steps towards me, but she stops him by putting her hand on his chest. The same hand that she's put on me at least a hundred times. I start to move forward, but I stop myself. "You would never do that," she whispers. She knows me better than anyone else and she's right. I wouldn't keep Blade away from her, but I won't let her know that. I want her to think that I'm a bastard. Maybe then she will think twice about jumping into bed with my brother.

"Try me, princess," I sneer. Her eyes widen, but this time she doesn't say anything back to me. I watch defeat wash over her expression and she moves her hand from his chest. "Bring him by the clubhouse later." She doesn't say anything, and I turn on my heel and walk away. Making my way towards my room, I punch the wall just inside the hallway.

I hate how fuckin' hostile she makes me. I want to do more than punch a damn wall, but I can't. I have other shit I need to handle, and I have a feeling that Romeo is going to find me when she leaves. Slamming my door, I walk into the bathroom and start the shower. The only thing I can think of right now is her, and I just hope I don't push her into the arms of Romeo.

After stripping down, I stand under the stream

and let the hot water coat my tense body. Every muscle is strained as I think about her walking away from me. Leaning my forehead against the shower wall, I stand there thinking about what she said. I hear the door open, and I don't even bother to turn around. The curtain moves, and I feel a body press against mine. It isn't Trix standing behind me, but my wife. Turning towards her, I look down into her eyes. The water coats her blonde hair, and she looks more like the woman I married all those years ago than the bitch I've lived with for the last ten.

"What do you want?" I ask. She doesn't say a word in response, but instead she grips my dick in her palm and slowly runs her hand up and down it. Closing my eyes, I lean back against the shower and I just feel her. We haven't been close in a long damn time and, even though I'm spitting mad at her, I don't say no. Yeah, I'm a bastard, but I've never claimed to be a better man.

Opening my eyes, I see the look in her eyes. She is trying to make it up to me for the shit she did. "Nothing you say or do is going to get you off my shit list. I won't change my mind. You try and get between me and Trix again, and I won't hesitate to kill you." My hand cups her cheek before it moves to grip her neck. I squeeze it hard enough to cut her oxygen off. Her eyes widen, and she starts to freak out. Her hands claw at my chest. Leaning towards her ear, I whisper, "Don't fuck with me." Releasing her, I push her towards the other side of the shower before I turn the water off and get out.

I hear her gasping for air, but I don't care. She could drop dead, and I wouldn't bat an eye. Making my way back out of the bathroom, I see Trix sitting on the bed. Her eyes eat me up, and I see her blush. "What are you doing here?" I ask.

Tina's voice cuts through the room and I see Trix flinch. "E, I need a towel." She turns the corner and she's still fuckin' naked. Trix jumps up off the bed, and tries to walk towards the door, but I don't let her move past me. When Tina notices that we are not alone, she grins and starts to walk towards us.

"Bitch, I bet you wish you had a body like mine." She runs her hands down her body and I shake my head. This bitch is delusional. I hate her body; it's like a damn twig that I was afraid that I'd break. When I was eighteen, her body was the fuckin' best thing I'd ever seen, but today the only body I like under mine is Trix's. Her curves make me feel like I'm actually fuckin' a woman and not a board.

"Get fuckin' dressed, and get the hell out. I already warned you and I ain't changing my mind," I bark out. She flinches slightly, rubbing her neck. I can see the bruise already starting to form. She huffs and makes her way back into the bathroom.

Turning my attention back to Trix, I watch her. Her eyes never leave the bathroom door, and I have a feeling that she's going to either go off on me or she's going to threaten to keep Blade from me. Maybe she'll even surprise me by telling me that she's fuckin' Romeo.

When Tina appears in the bathroom doorway, I see the way she's looking at Trix. If looks could kill, we'd both be dead right now. She walks past us and runs her shoulder into my arm before walking out the door and into the hall. The door slams closed with a loud bang, and I'm just glad she's gone.

"Did you fuck her?" Her question surprises me. I didn't think that she would actually care who I fucked since she told me she was done. What she doesn't fuckin' know is that I haven't slept with my wife in over three years. Partly because I'm never fuckin' home anymore, and partly because the only woman I wanted in my bed is the one standing right in front of me.

"Does she look like I fucked her?" She shakes her head no, and her eyes meet mine. They bore into me with an angry glare and I inch closer to her. Grabbing her around the waist, I pull her to my naked body. Her body instantly tenses, but I don't release my grip on her. Just seeing her makes my dick harden, and I'm pretty sure she's very aware of what she does to me.

"That's not what I'm here for," she says, tersely. Looking at her, I watch her expressions before I ask her why she's here. They change from scared, hurt, happy, and sad all in the matter of seconds. "Can you get dressed?" she asks, sounding put out by having to be with me while I'm naked. A few days ago, she wouldn't have asked me to get dressed. She would have been naked right there with me. I would have her riding on my dick by now.

"What did you come back here for? The sooner you spit it the fuck out, the sooner you don't have to be around my naked dick." Her eyes travel their way down to my dick, and she bites her lip slightly. Grabbing my dick, I stroke it a few times and watch as her lips part.

My dick jutting out between us, I grab her and pull her body to mine. Leaning forward, I claim her mouth like it's going to be my last time. It probably will be with the way shit is going between us. Grabbing her ass, I rub her against my hard dick and she moans at the sensations. Picking her up, I walk us the rest of the way to the bed and lay her down. I take my time running my mouth up and down her neck, sucking and nipping my way towards her cleavage. Grabbing the bottom of her tank top, I pull it up and over her head, tossing it to the ground.

My mouth trails over every inch of her skin, memorizing it. Her moans and gasps tell me exactly what she likes, and I reach around her to undo her bra. Once I free her amazing fuckin' tits, I lavish each nipple and suck on them. Her legs wrap around my hips, and I know that she's too far gone to stop me now. She thinks I don't own her body, but she is dead fuckin' wrong.

Releasing her nipple from my teeth, I scoot back on the bed and start to work on her jeans. Pulling them down her thighs, I kiss my way down her belly and make my way to her pussy. Before I get her jeans off of her, I run my finger through her slit just to see how wet she is.

Pulling her jeans the rest of the way down, I toss them on the ground and get between her legs. Angling my dick at her opening, I pause before I slam home. "You'll never get this wet for him. I own your fuckin' body, and he will never make you feel the way I do." She goes to say something, but I shut her up when I slam into her. Her fingers dig into my skin and her eyes close.

"Oh my god," she whimpers. "Elec." No one ever calls me by my whole name. Either they say it fuckin' wrong or I don't give it to them. Trix is one of the only people who calls me that anymore, my given name, the name that my son shares: Elec Blade.

We fuck long and hard until she's screaming out my name. I hope that smug bastard hears her. And I hope it fuckin' eats away at him, knowing that he will never be nothing more than a replacement for the real fuckin' thing. He will never own her the way I do.

Coming inside of her, I slow my rhythm and collapse on top of her spent body. She doesn't try to push me off, and I don't even bother moving. I want to stay buried inside of her for as long as I can. Her hands slowly start to run along the back of my head and her nails scratch against my scalp. Her fingers tangle in the short hair at the top, and she gives it a slight tug.

My fingertip runs over her nipple over and over again until I watch it pebble. Her body breaks out in chills, and I can't help but grin. Biting her other tit, I soothe it with my tongue before she says anything else. "This still doesn't change anything." Her voice is a somber whisper. "You had her in your room while you were both naked. Elec, I don't even know what to think. You probably fucked her and now I'm stupid enough to fuck you, too." She shakes her head against the sheets, and I watch as a tear slips down the side of her eye.

"I haven't fucked her since I promised you that I was leaving her." Her frown tells me that she doesn't believe me and there is nothing I can do to prove it to her. "You are the only bitch I'm fuckin'. The only one I've fucked in three years. The only one I want to fuck."

"Yet, you are still married. How the fuck do you think that makes me feel? Huh? I feel like I don't mean shit to you and, in reality, I don't. You couldn't even leave your wife." She closes her eyes for a second before she opens them again, tears shining in them. "You promised me a forever, and all I've gotten were broken promises and lies. I look like an idiot to the guys out there and I'll never be more than your whore. At least Rom-"

I stop her before she can say his name and ruin everything else between us. "Don't you dare say his name while I'm inside of you. You have my cum between your thighs and inside of you. You want this shit to end, fine. Leave. Walk out that door. Just know that I'll always be the only fucker who makes you feel alive." She pushes me off of her, and I lean back on my arms to watch her get dressed.

"You're such a bastard. I don't know why I ever fell in love with you!" she spits, as she pulls on her jeans.

"You and I both know why. Same reason I fell in love with you." Her whole body pauses and she looks over at me. In the three years that we've been together, I never once told her I loved her. Call me fuckin' stupid if you want, but I couldn't. Not after shit with Tina and the way she manipulated the words I said for her own benefit.

"You love me?" she asks. Her tank is around her arms, but she hasn't pulled it over her head yet.

"I didn't fuckin' stutter." Her mouth drops open in shock, but her brain catches up with her mouth, and she finishes pulling on her tank. Once she has her flip-flops on, she makes her way towards the bed to grab her bag and darts for the door.

"You don't know how to love." I want to say her

words hurt, but they don't. She's probably right.

"I may not be the best at showing someone how I fuckin' feel, but that doesn't mean shit. Bring my son to the clubhouse later." She scoffs at my angry tone and she turns on her heel. Before she can walk out the door, she turns back towards me.

"You're such a fuckin' dick. I feel sorry for the bastard you've become."

"You're the one who has to deal with me." She frowns, and then I say something that is going to piss her off even more. "Bitch, I hope you get pregnant again. Then, we will see how much of a bastard I am when you have two kids from me." Her cheeks flush red with anger. She flips me the bird before swinging the door open and letting it slam against the wall with a loud crash.

I watch her ass shake as she makes her way away from me. If she doesn't bring my son to me, I'll just go to her.

Chapter Two

Two months. Two days. Five hours.

She still won't fuckin' talk to me and, to be honest, I miss the fuck out of her. She was always the one to keep my head on straight when it came to the club. She kept me stress free by sucking my dick at any given time, and letting me take my aggressions out on her body when I fucked her raw. One look in her eyes was all it took to bring me back from the ledge.

Looking down at my phone, I see a new message from her. That is what we've become. Single fuckin' text messages that let me know she's bringing Blade by the clubhouse. She doesn't say a word to me when she gets here, and doesn't say a word when she picks him up the next day. All she does is toss the fuckin' diaper bag at me and sets him on the bed. There is no getting close to her, because she just won't let me. To say she's fuckin' pissed is an understatement, but I don't regret a word I said.

A knock at the door twenty minutes later alerts me to them being here. Getting up off my bed, I open the door and she shoves the diaper bag at me, pushing me inside the room. She doesn't say a word to me and, when I look down at her belly, I can't help but smile. She isn't leaving without us talking this time.

Every week, we do the same damn game. I check her stomach for any signs that I knocked her up again and she glares at me. This week is the first that I'm noticing a change in the way her jeans fit more snuggly around her ass, the way her tee shirt clings to her larger breasts and her slightly swollen stomach. I remember exactly the way she looked when I found out she was pregnant. She told me it was mine from day one, but I didn't believe her back then. I still fucked her every day, and anytime she wanted a piece of me, because she was my drug. It didn't change the fact that she was a club whore and fucked all the brothers. That kid could have been anyone's.

She sets Blade on the bed, and turns to walk right back out the door, but I grab her wrist and stop her. Her eyes widen at the contact and she tries to pull herself out of my grip. "Don't fuckin' fight me," I growl in her ear. It doesn't stop her from trying like hell to get away from me.

"Let me go, Elec," she demands in a low voice.

"No. We need to talk." I motion to her stomach, and she pushes against my chest once more.

"We don't need to do anything. My life doesn't concern you." Some of the fight in her drains, but I don't let her walk away from me.

"If that's my kid then, yeah babe, I think it does." She shoots me a dirty look and I grin back at her. Just by her reaction, I know that I knocked her up again. I'm sure if it weren't mine, she would have been happy to put me in my place.

"It's not your business. You're married." She pulls her hand out of my grip, and I let her slowly walk towards the door.

"Married or not, if you lie to me, I'll make you

regret it." She pales for a second before she runs towards the bathroom. I make sure that Blade has his train toy in his hands before I go in after her. Her ass is in the air, as she throws up into the toilet. Her knees don't touch the ground, and that's probably a good thing. My bathroom is gross as fuck since she doesn't spend all her free time here with me anymore. Walking over to her, I grab her hair and hold it back from her face.

"You want to rethink your statement?" I ask.

She turns her head to look at me, and I can see the anger written all over her face. "Don't you know that I've been whoring all over town? How could it possibly be yours?" She wipes her mouth with some toilet paper and flushes the toilet. Releasing her hair, I watch her walk over to the sink to rinse her mouth out.

"You and I both know that isn't true. You haven't been here longer than enough time to drop off Blade. So, unless you've been fuckin' my VP since the last time we fucked, that kid is mine." Her brows furrow in anger, and she presses her finger into my chest.

"Fuck you." The tips of her ears turn pink, and she looks like she's about to blow a damn gasket. It's fuckin' hot when she gets all bent out of shape.

"He the father of your kid?" I ask in a low voice. She stares at me with just as much anger as I feel running though my veins. Before she can answer, I release her and storm out of the room. He's been sniffing around her way too damn long. Making my way into the bar area, I find him and stalk towards him. The few guys are that hanging around don't make a sound, as I get closer to Romeo.

"Have you been fuckin' her?" The anger just takes a hold of me, and there is nothing I can do to control it. He looks over my shoulder and, when I turn my attention to who he's looking at, I see Trix's face. She has Blade on her hip, and she has a look of disgust on her face. It should bother me that she's letting our son see this, but all my anger is being directed at Romeo.

When he turns his attention back to me, I stare into his eyes. "You really want to know how I've been taking her to bed every night?" He grins and I don't think twice. I swing hard and my fist connects with his cheekbone. I watch the way his head jerks to the side and I swing again.

Someone steps between us and, when I look up, I see Stavros standing there facing me. He looks pissed, but it isn't any different than how he's been since Harlyn walked out on his ass again. "Get the fuck out of here. I don't give a shit what your baby mama drama is. This shit is fuckin' over." I stare at Romeo over Stavros's shoulder as he wipes at his cheek and grins. "Go!" Stavros growls.

Turning my attention back to Trix, I make my way over to her and grab Blade out of her grasp. I don't give her the opportunity to say anything before I stalk off.

Walking into my room, I slam the door shut and Blade starts to cry. Closing my eyes, I run my hand up and down his back trying to soothe him. "I'm sorry, little man. Your momma just pisses me off so damn bad."

Reaching into the bag on my bed, I grab his bottle and mix the water and formula like Trix showed me. Handing the bottle to him, he starts to drink and I take a seat on my bed and watch his features. Every time she brings Blade over, it's his naptime and I almost think she does this just to piss me off. I lose an hour or two every damn time.

When he's almost done with his bottle, his little eyes start to close and I just watch him. He's breathtaking and by far the best damn thing I've ever done.

Shit with Tina still isn't getting better, but I finally got those fuckin' CPS fuckers off our backs. They made us jump through hoops to prove that Blade was well cared for and that there were no signs of abuse. I could kill that bitch.

His little feet start to kick like he's running in his dream, and I can't help but think about the type of sleeper his mom is. Every time I've had Trix in my bed, she's done the same feet movements. Maybe it's something in the genetics, but it's cute as hell. A soft knock at the door brings my attention to it, and I see Trix peek her head inside.

"What Trixibella?" I murmur, running my

fingers down Blade's sweet chubby face. She walks in and shuts the door softly.

"I haven't heard you call me that in a long time." Her eyes are cast down towards the ground and she almost looks nervous.

"What do you want?" I ask again. I just want to spend time with my son, and there is no fuckin' way I want to hear about her and Romeo.

"Elec…" she starts and pauses, almost like she doesn't know what to say to me. She has to know how fuckin' pissed I am at her right now. She's fuckin' my brother.

"Trixibella, I don't have time for your shit. You haven't talked to me in months and now you want to say something? Well, spit it the fuck out. It's my time with our son and I don't need your ass hanging around any longer than necessary." Blade moves at my words, but he doesn't open his eyes. Laying him in the crease of my legs, I turn my attention back to her.

"I didn't mean for it to happen." She looks at the floor, and I don't know if she means the getting pregnant part or the fuckin' Romeo part. "Honestly, I don't know whose baby it is." She closes her eyes and my hands itch to go to her. When she opens them and looks at me, I see the tears pooling in her eyes.

"You didn't mean to fuck him? What happened, you just fell naked on his dick?" She glares at me, but I keep going. "What's going to happen when he finds out it's not his kid, or hell it's not even mine? You just going to keep whoring yourself out to anyone who says they give a fuck about you?" Her eyes meet mine and, for the first time in a long time, I see regret.

"Elec. I already feel bad enough. You don't have to be a bastard," she whispers.

"You fuck him bareback, too?" The hurt in her eyes flashes bright and she frowns at my question.

"No. We used protection almost every time." She looks down at our son, but doesn't make a move to come closer. I can see the need to hold him written all over her face.

"What do you want?" I ask. It may sound like a simple question, but for us it's nothing but complicated.

"I don't know…" I don't even bother to look at

her this time. It's probably going to piss me off.

"You want the baby to be his?" I'm still watching Blade because hearing her answer might be the end of us for good this time.

"I… I… Elec…" She starts to move closer to me and, when I look up at her, she stops. Her eyes stare into mine, and I wait for her to answer. When she doesn't give me anything, I ask her another question.

"Is he who you want to be with? I'll walk away right now, and let you go, if that's what you really want. You say the word and I won't come back." My eyes pin her to the spot she's standing, and I watch as tears fall down her face.

"What about Blade?" Her voice is choked up, and I want nothing more than to kill that bastard Romeo for taking my place in her heart.

"I'll visit him. He'll always be my son, and there is nothing that will change that." I look past her towards the wall, and I ask her to do something for me real quick. "Can you watch him for a second? There is something I need to do." She nods slightly, looking a little worried.

Getting off the bed, I walk over to her and kiss the top of her head before making my way towards the door. "What are you doing?" She asks with tears in her eyes.

"I'm giving you what you want. You and Romeo can be happy together." I turn before she can stop me again and make my way out of the room and towards Prez's office. Knocking on the door, I wait for him to answer and then make my way inside.

"You gonna tell me what the fuck happened before?" he asks from behind his desk.

"She's pregnant," I state. I don't even bother to say anything else. He knows exactly what is running through my mind because he is going through the same damn thing. Harlyn still isn't talking to him, and she's pregnant with his kid.

"It yours?" he asks.

I shrug and sink into a chair across from him. "No fuckin' clue. She doesn't even know." I close my eyes, and lean my head back against the chair. "I want to leave this charter and go nomad. I can't watch them together. There is no fuckin' way. It will just eat me alive if I have to watch him touch my girl."

He regards me for a while before he responds to my request. "Does she know this is what you're doing?"

"Doesn't matter. I'll visit with my son, and all that shit, but I can't be here." He nods and I sigh. "I love this club more than anything, but losing her to him isn't ever going to mesh well for me. I'll never trust the fucker again. He knows exactly how I feel about her, and he still made his move behind my back."

"You know this has to go through a vote." I nod and go to stand up. "I'm sorry to see you go, but I understand, brother. I wouldn't fuckin' be able to stomach watching if my girl was with another one of you bastards either. I'll schedule church for after she comes to get Blade tomorrow." I nod and reach out my hand to shake his. He didn't have to agree to give me the meeting, especially after the shit in the bar.

Walking out the door, I make my way back towards my room where I'll get to spend at least one more night with my son before my fate is sealed. When I walk into the room, I see her sitting on my bed against the wall with our son curled up in her arms. Her eyes are closed and, when I shut the door, she doesn't even move. Looks like my fate is already sealed. I get both of them in my bed one last time.

Chapter Three

Waking up with an ass pressed tightly against my dick isn't what I was expecting this morning, but I will take what I can get. Before I even realize that it's Trix in my arms, I'm running my fingers down the soft skin of her belly towards the top of her panties. I feel the slight swell of her abdomen and my hand pauses. She pushes her ass back into me, and my hand slides down into her panties. She must have taken her jeans off sometime during the night.

Cupping her pussy, I don't even bother thinking about the consequences of my actions. She'll be pissed at me and herself in a few minutes, but the only thing I can think of is the feel of my fingers sliding into her juices.

Kissing her neck, I look over her towards the crib I got for Blade when we started these overnight visits. He's still fast asleep with his finger in his mouth. She moans into the quiet room, and I slide her panties to the side. Dipping my fingers inside of her, I feel her pussy grip me tightly. Pregnant pussy is the best damn pussy.

My hand goes around her throat, and I pull her back into my body. Sliding my sweats down enough to get my dick out, I rub it between her wetness and slide it over her clit causing her to moan out my name. "Elec."

She knows it's me, and part of that makes me feel like there might be hope for us. Sinking inside of her, I slowly thrust in and out of her. My grip on her neck tightens, but not enough to leave marks on her skin. My other hand slowly makes its way over her belly. God, I wish this was my kid, too. I want to be the only man to ever be the father of her children.

We fuck slowly until we both come. Her pussy clenches around me tighter than ever before as she moans out. It's a goodbye of sorts. I'm not sure she understood my meaning last night when I told her that I'd walk away if she chose him. Today, when they leave and if my request is granted, I'm leaving. I'm filing for divorce from Tina, and I'm getting the fuck out of this town.

That bitch will no longer run my damn life. I'll finally be free of all of her drama and most importantly… her.

I feel a tear hit my skin. When I pull out of Trix, she turns in my arms and I see the tears in her eyes. "Elec… We shouldn't…" I put my finger to her lips to stop her from talking.

"Don't. Don't regret it. Just know that whatever happens, I love you. I've loved you for the last three years, and I never meant to break my promise to you. Trixibella, don't forget what we had even when it was fucked up and crazy. Know that it was the only time I've been truly happy. I love you and Blade more than life itself, and I just want you happy, even if it kills me." I place one last kiss on her lips before I slide out of bed and fix my sweats.

Walking over to Blade, I press a kiss to his

forehead and watch him for a minute before I walk into the bathroom to shower. I take the longest and hottest shower I can manage. I don't hear her, so I assume that she still isn't gone yet. I wonder what that bastard Romeo is going to think when he sees her coming out of my room wearing the same clothes as yesterday. Once I'm done in the shower, I shut the water off and towel dry. Tossing it on the curtain, I make my way back to my room to see her still sitting on my bed.

She's fully clothed when I make it over to the bed and her eyes are trained on the floor. She doesn't even move when I take a seat next to her. Before I can even say one word to her, my phone rings out with a message.

Prez: ***Church. Now.***

Taking a deep breath, I toss my phone on the bed and walk naked over to my dresser to pull on a pair of jeans. My eye catches on the divorce papers I filled out two years ago. I reach forward and touch them, but I don't move them from their resting place. I had every intention of taking them to the club lawyer, but then Tina threatened to commit suicide. She was still my wife, and I couldn't let her take her own life because of me.

Instead, I broke the heart of the woman who matters the most to me. I'm a coward and a bastard, this much I know. Letting that bitch run my life was the worst mistake I ever made. Pulling on socks and my boots next, I look over at the crib to see Blade's eyes open. He reaches out his hand to me, and I grin at him.

Even with this shit that is going on, he never fails to put a smile on my face. "Dadda," he coos into the quiet room. I hear Trix's gasp at his word and, when I turn my face to look at her, she has a look of shock written all over her face.

"He's never said a word before," she whispers. My eyebrows bunch in confusion and I look back at him before looking at Trix one more time. "You're his first word." A tear slides down her cheek and I walk over to him and pick him up.

"Hey, buddy." His hand comes to my face, so I grab it with my free hand and pull it to my mouth. He has no fuckin' clue what I would do for him.

He starts to do his baby talk thing where you

can't understand a damn thing that is coming out of his mouth and I hand him over to Trix. "I have church in a minute." She takes him without a word, and starts to make his bottle.

Everything she does with him is effortless. I watch as she cuddles him into her body and hands him his bottle. He watches her and me as he drinks it. Pulling on a shirt and my cut, I take a look around the room. In the next ten to fifteen minutes, I'll know my fate. I have a feeling they will give me what I want in order to keep the peace between the club.

"Come on, I'll walk you out." I reach a hand out to her and she stares at it for a minute. "It's not like I'll say anything to the bastard," I state when she doesn't move. Her eyes roam over my body before landing back on my outstretched hand.

She takes my hand, and I pull them both up from the bed. I grab the diaper bag and shove everything back inside. Leading them towards the door, I open it and lead them out into the hall. The silence consumes me, and I have a feeling that everyone is already in church. Making our way through the quiet room, I see Prez and Romeo standing together by the church door.

Neither of them says anything as I lead Trix and Blade outside and towards her car. Once I get them settled in the car, and I give him one last kiss on the cheek, I pull away and watch as she starts the car and takes off into the morning light. Closing my eyes, I stand there for a second as my decision weights on my mind.

I'm going to be leaving them both in the matter of hours. She doesn't know, either. As much as I want to pick up the phone and call her to tell her, I don't. I just let her keep driving further away from me.

Making my way back into the clubhouse, I see the look on Romeo's face. He's pissed, and I'm pretty damn sure he knows that she stayed with me last night. The church doors are closed, and Prez is nowhere in sight.

"Why?" His voice is on edge and, as much as I want to fuck with him, I don't.

"Because I love her enough to walk away," I state. He rolls his eyes at me, and takes a few steps closer.

"Is that why she spent the night in your bed last night?" he sneers. "You trying to prove to her one last time that you're the one for her." I shake my head and laugh.

"No fuck head. I didn't even ask her to stay. She fell asleep before I even got back to my room. Could I have sent her away? Yeah, probably, but I wanted to see the look on your face when you saw her doing the walk of shame from my room one last time." Before I even finish the statement, his fist clocks me in the side of my jaw.

I don't bother hitting him back because the door to church opens, and I see Prez standing there watching us. "Get your asses in here. We don't have all fuckin' day." I rub at my jaw and follow orders. When I take my seat at the table, I sit in silence as everyone's eyes are on me. Prez already told them what I was asking for. The only thing left is to vote.

"We ready to vote on E's fate?" he asks the room. I hear a smart-ass remark from Romeo, but I shake it off. I just need a majority and I'm gone.

One by one, I hear the yay's until two of the brothers say nay. My eyes meet them, and they're the ones I've been friends with since we prospected together. I don't say anything, but I continue to listen to all the rest of the votes until it comes to Romeo and Prez. Romeo says nay and so does Prez. Surprising. "I'd rather you watch as I fuck your girl," Romeo spits out.

"You'd like that, wouldn't you? What are you going to do, adopt my kid, too?" I ask with a bitter laugh.

"You'll never see him again," he laughs.

He doesn't know she's pregnant and, although I want to let that fuckin' cat out of the bag, I don't. I'll keep that one in my arsenal for when I come back to see my boy. "Keep him from me and you'll wish you never laid eyes on her." Prez hits the gavel on the table, and every one turns their attention to him.

"Enough. You fuckers act like goddamn children." He runs his hand over his short beard, and I wait for him to give the ruling. Once church is done, I'm packing my shit and leaving.

"Although I hate this shit, the majority rules and, in this case, Easy E you are now a nomad. Be sure you come to visit and don't forget your brothers here. I wish you nothing but the best, and I hope you and Trix figure out your shit for Blade's sake." I nod to him and wait for him to dismiss us. When the gavel hits the table again, I bounce out of my seat and make a beeline towards the door. Before I can get through it, a hand grabs my arm.

Turning to face Prez, I look him in the eye and wait for him to speak his peace. The room clears and I watch as all the brothers pass us, including Romeo. He runs his shoulder into me and, as I turn to punch the fucker, Prez stops me. He closes the door behind the last brother to leave and he motions to the chairs. Taking a seat, I wait for him to say his peace.

"You're running like a pussy. Why the fuck are you not taking your girl back?" I shrug and keep from saying a word. "This isn't like you, E. I've known you a long while now, and you know she's pregnant again. That kid could be yours, and you're just going to let someone else come in and step up to be that child's father?"

"It could be his. Who the fuck knows?" I reply, shrugging my shoulders again. He shakes his head and taps his fingers on the table.

"You're not just trying to skip town on raising your kid are you?"

"Fuck no. I'll be back to see him as much as she lets me. I'll send her money whenever she needs. I just have shit I need to take care of before I can even think about settling down anywhere." He raises an eyebrow at me and I continue. "I'm filing for divorce, and I'll deal with the shit storm that I already know I'll be dealing with because of her bullshit."

"About damn time, fucker." He doesn't say anything else even though I know he wants to. He dismisses me with a look, and I get up from my chair. Walking towards the door, I put my hand on the doorknob and look over my shoulder at him.

"Thanks, Prez. I know I don't deserve shit for the way I've treated her, but I will make it up to them both." He nods and sits back in his chair. Opening the door, I make my way out of the room and towards my room.

Chapter Four

One month. Three Days. Ten hours.

The beeping of my phone jolts me awake. Cursing under my breath, I pull my arm out from under the bitch I fucked earlier and turn on the screen. The bright light almost blinds me. My eyes burn and, when I look down at the name on the screen, I feel like I got sucker punched. She has been texting me every damn day since she found out I left the club to go nomad. It was over a month ago. She always wants to know where the fuck I am and when I'll be coming home.

The only time I stick around in town is when I have Blade. She lets me have him for three days at a time and, even then, she is always up my damn ass like she was my damn wife. Only I don't get any of the damn benefits anymore.

Home. I don't have a home anymore. That bitch Tina set my fuckin' house on fire when the club's lawyers served her the divorce papers. The only thing that I own anymore is my bike and that fuckin' bitch is trying to take even that in the divorce.

Trixibella: ***E, I need you to call me. Please?***

Laying my head back on the shitty mattress that this bitch owns, I blow out a breath. Why the fuck does she want me to call her at midnight? Hitting the button to make my phone call her, I put the phone to my ear and wait for her to answer.

"Elec," she whispers.

"What babe?" I ask, throwing my arm over my eyes to block out some of the light coming in from the other room. There is music still blasting through the small ass house, and it sounds like the party is still just as fuckin' hopping as it was when I took this bitch to bed.

"I need you." Her voice breaks and it causes my spine to straighten. What the fuck does she mean she needs me?

"What are you talking about, babe?" Either I'm still fuckin' hammered or those words really came out of her mouth.

"I messed it all up E. I… I…" She can't get the words out and, instead of being fuckin' smart, I get out of the bitch's grip from earlier and pull my jeans on. Searching for my shirt, I pull my boots on and wait for her to spit it the fuck out.

"I told him about the baby and he left. He won't return my calls, and I don't know what to do." She finally stutters out. "E." I hear Blade cry in the background, and I mutter out a fuck.

"You at the apartment?" I ask. I know it's fuckin' stupid, but I would still do anything for this bitch. She could call me a millions times in the middle of the night, and I'd still come running like a goddamn idiot.

"Yeah." I hear her try and sooth Blade, but he is inconsolable.

"I'm on my way. I'll be there in twenty." I hang up before she can say anything and pocket my phone. Before I can even get out of the damn room, my phone is ringing again. Looking at the screen, this time I see Romeo's name on the screen. Just fuckin' great.

"Yeah?" I answer. At least now I'm fuckin' awake.

"I should have fucking known that you had something else up your goddamn sleeve. The kid is yours, isn't it?" I smirk, and make my way through the party. When I get to the door, I open it and walk into the crisp night air.

"Who the fuck knows? She doesn't know and maybe if you didn't fuck one of your brothers' women you wouldn't be in this shit. But, right now, I know that I had a panicked woman call me and my son was screaming in the background. Maybe pulling that disappearing act you're so fuckin' good at would have been better if I had my son for the night." I walk over to my bike and straddle her.

"You think you're going to put her back together again, asshole? You're not. You and I both know that her heart belongs to me and there is no way in hell that it will ever be yours. So, try all you fuckin' want but, in the end, she'll be back in my bed sucking my dick." I hang up before he can even say a reply. Making the long drive to her apartment, I get there record time. Parking my bike, I scan the area and see that he still hasn't made it back here. Either he's a bigger idiot than I thought, or he's that fuckin' pissed.

Walking up to her door, I can hear Blade screaming though the thin walls. This place is shit for privacy. I gently knock on the door before grabbing the key she gave me a while back. Unlocking the door, I see her rocking him in the middle of the living room. Wet angry tears are streaming down his face and, when he sees me, he reaches out for me. Shutting the door and locking it behind me, I make my way towards them and take him from her arms.

"Thank God, you finally got here. He's been screaming since we got off the phone." He quiets in my arms, and I wipe his cheeks.

"What's wrong?" I ask, studying her face.

She sighs and walks away from me. "I don't even know what I'm doing anymore. Blade is never happy when you aren't here, and Romeo is pissed that I don't know whose kid this is." She points to her belly, and I want to reach out and touch her. Even if it isn't my kid, I'd still raise it as my own. Who the fuck am I kidding? I want this kid to be mine, too.

"Tell him it's mine and be done with his sorry ass," I say. I rub my hand down Blade's back as he tucks his face into my neck. Taking a seat on the tiny ass fuckin' couch that she owns, I make it look like it's from a damn dollhouse.

"E." She says it on a sigh. I look over at her, and watch the panic start to take over her features.

"He called me," I state. Blade starts to climb all over me, and I keep him from falling off the couch.

"Dadda," he giggles, when I grab his hand as he starts to fall. I catch him before he falls and Trix turns her attention to me.

"What do you mean he called you?" She gives me a dirty look and I frown. I don't get why she fuckin' cares what the fucker called about.

"He thinks I've got something up my sleeve. I told him that I didn't do shit, and that I didn't know whose kid it is." She frowns and takes a seat next to me. She reaches over to grab Blade's hand and kisses it. His eyes close, and he tucks his head into my arm.

"I'm going to put him in bed." I start to stand up and she slowly lets go of him. Walking him into his room, I lay him in his bed. Putting his blanket over him, I tuck him in and press a kiss on his forehead. His fingers curl around mine, and I can't help but smile. My love for this little boy grows immensely every day that I spend time with him.

After spending a few minutes watching him, I turn to leave the room and see Trix standing in the doorway watching me. "You're amazing with him," she whispers.

I nod my head and walk past her. When I turn around, I see her walk into the room and run her hand over his hair before she kisses him and makes her way towards me. She stops next to me, and I wrap my arm around her waist. "Elec…" her voice trails off and I see the way her eyes light up. Her feelings for me have never changed, and we both know it. She tries to make me think she could give a fuck less about me, but we both know the truth.

She wants me just as bad as I want her. I pull her

body to mine. Leaning down, I press my mouth to hers. She kisses be back roughly for a few minutes before she pulls away and puts her fingers to her lips. "I can't, E. Not with the way things are between me and-" I stop her from saying his fuckin' name.

I hate that damn bastard. I start walking towards the front door, but she stops me. "E." Her voice stops me dead in my tracks. When I turn to look at her, I see the uncertainty written all over her face. "Please stay. I would hate for you to go and sleep in a shitty hotel while you're in town. I was the one who called and brought you here in the middle of the night. It's the least I can do."

I shake my head and go to open the door. I can't stay here and keep my hands off of her. "Trust me baby, if I stay, we would wind up in bed together." She frowns, and I start to move again. "I'll come by in the next few days to pick up our boy."

She nods, and I shut the door behind me. Making my way to my bike, I make the mistake of looking back one last time. Her face is in the window, and I see her wipe at her eyes. Straddling my bike, I crank the engine and ride away from my life.

Making my way towards the hotel I typically stay at when I'm in town, I see that bitch Tina strutting down the main drag by the bars. Her blonde hair is fluffed up on top of her head in a rat's nest-looking thing, and I slow to a stop next to her. "I thought you'd be fucking your whore still." She raises a perfectly done eyebrow, and I can't help but laugh at her ass.

"I fuck who I want, when I want," I grin.

She snorts at my words, and I wait for her response. "You mean she got smart and left your stupid ass, too. I heard the rumors going around and how she's pregnant again. She spreads her legs more than the average whore."

Getting off my bike, I stalk towards her and back her up against the building. The darkness keeps us hidden from any prying eyes, and I'm sure it looks like I'm about to fuck her in the dark corner. "You say another thing to bad mouth the mother of my child, and I won't hesitate to put you down like the bitch you are." Her eyes flash with anger, and she reaches out to slap me, but I grab her hand and force it behind her back.

"You don't scare me, you pussy. A real man doesn't step out on his wife." I lean in closer to her and her body melts to mine. She doesn't mean a damn word she says. I still light up her body like I did for years.

"A wife wouldn't make her ol' man's life so miserable that he would do whatever it took to get the fuck away from her either. So, before you start spewing the same shit you've been trying to spew at me for years, I suggest you take a damn look in the mirror." She huffs and I push away from her. I get back on my bike and start the engine just as the bitch comes launching herself at me, screaming her damn head off.

"You smug bastard. You are the only reason our fucking marriage didn't work! You were too busy screwing that damn whore to give a damn about me." A few people stop and stare at her fuckin' outburst. She hits me a few times, and I have to fight to keep the bike and me upright. "You had a fucking child with that bitch," she says on a sob. Some guy notices me trying to keep the bike up, and he pulls her off of me. Putting the kickstand down, I get off my bike and make my way towards her.

Her eyes are now filling with angry tears, and she's yelling at the guy for pulling her crazy ass off of me. He flips her the bird and nods in my direction. "Tina, chill the fuck out. Our marriage didn't work because we are both selfish fuckin' people. I only married you because you gave me an ultimatum, and I liked the way you sucked my dick. I should have fuckin' walked out that door years before I started stepping out on you. Yeah, I'm a bastard for that, but I don't regret a damn thing I did with Trix. You threatening to commit suicide is the only reason I stuck around the last two years. Otherwise I'd be living the fuckin' life I want with my son and my girl." The crowd around us doesn't move, and they are listening to every damn word, but I don't give a fuck. She needs to hear this shit apparently.

"Bitch, you set our damn house on fire when I

had my lawyer deliver the divorce papers. You're fuckin' crazy and I'm glad that I'm ridding myself of you. I lost a lot being a bastard to you, and I'm sorry for that, but coming at me and screaming at me isn't going to change the fact that we don't work. We never have and never will. Stay the fuck away from my son, his mother, and me. You'll regret it if you don't."

Her mouth just opens and closes without any noises coming from her. I walk over to my bike and mount it before I take off into the night towards the hotel. Once I check in, I make my way to the room and swing the door open. I've had enough of the fuckin' drama tonight. I just want to start over and make choices that would land my girl and me back together. Trixibella and I would be settled down with a family and shit if I wasn't a fuckin' idiot. I would know without a doubt that that kid is mine.

Chapter Five

Six months. Two weeks. Three Days.

My divorce is finally fuckin' over and I can start fresh. Every week, like clockwork, I check into a hotel and my Trixibella stops by to bring me my son. Tonight is going to be the first time that she brings him to my house. I bought it a few days after I got word that my divorce would be final. It's not much, but it's enough for me to get by with.

A knock at the door brings me to my feet. Walking over to it, I see the door open and my little man comes running as fast as his little chubby legs can bring him. He trips and falls to the carpet and looks up at me with alligator tears that don't work on me like they do his mom. He starts to cry just as I scoop him up and press a kiss to his cheek.

"Hey, buddy. You can run now." He nods his head, and I wipe the tears off his cheek.

"Dadda." He whimpers. "I urt." I hold him so I can kiss his hurt knee, and he grabs my face in both of his small hands and starts to giggle. He's resilient. He can cut his leg up, causing him to cry for a minute, before he starts to laugh and do something else that will get him hurt.

I hear her giggle and when I look up, I get the breath knocked out of me. She's fuckin' beautiful. Even at nine months pregnant, I still can't help but stare at her. "Elec," she says with a smile. She's glowing with happiness and I know it's not because of me.

"Hey, Trixibella. You look fuckin' beautiful." She waddles closer to me, and I press my lips to her cheek. She blushes and I hate knowing that she will be going back to him in just a few short minutes.

"Stavros said you're coming back?" Her voice practically brings me to my knees. I want nothing more than to listen to her whisper all the dirty things she wants to do to me like she used to.

"Depends," I say shrugging. She arches an eyebrow at me, waiting for me to continue. "You already know I won't come back while you're still together. I can't watch that fuckin' shit. You're mine, baby." She shakes her head, and her red hair bounces around her shoulders.

"E, we've been over this a hundred times. I'm happy." She doesn't say it very convincingly.

"You don't look all that happy." I state. Blade forces me to let him go, and he starts to run towards the couch. She hands me his bag, and I watch as she waddles her way towards the couch. She slowly sits down, and I watch her expression change. She hunches over in pain and cries out.

Closing the distance between us, I grab her hand and she squeezes the shit out of it. "E," she pants out. "I think..." She stops and squeezes harder. "I'm going into labor," she finally pants out. I get out of her grip and grab Blade. Helping Trix off of the couch, I help her out to the car and get her into the passenger seat. Grabbing my phone from my pocket, I dial Prez's number and tell him to meet us at the hospital. I don't care if Romeo might be this kids dad, I won't be the one calling his ass. Plus Prez is the only one I trust Blade with.

After I get Blade strapped into the seat, I shut the door and make my way to the driver's side. We make our way to the hospital with her squeezing the shit out of my hand the whole way.

When I pull into a spot, I turn the car off, and make my way to her door and open it. A nurse comes running towards us with a wheelchair, and I can only thank that fucker Stavros for being a lot calmer than me about this shit. I grab Blade and we follow her into the hospital. After they get her into a room, and shit all set up, they kick Blade and I out until I can get someone to take him while she gives birth.

I see Prez come jogging towards us, and he reaches out and takes Blade before I can even say anything. He motions for me to go, and I run back towards the room that they kicked me out from earlier. When I get back inside, they toss some scrub like things at me and tell me to get dressed before I come closer to her. Once I get that shit on, I walk over to her and grab her hand. She has sweat pouring down her face, and her face is contorted in discomfort.

"E. I hate you so bad right now," she whimpers. I press a kiss to her sweaty forehand and grin.

"You can hate me all you want, but just know that I love you." She starts to whimper as a doctor comes into the room.

"You are ready to push, Trix," the doctor states. Trix grabs my hand, and squeezes it harder than all the other times as she screams out.

"I fucking hate you, Elec," she screams on the second push. Like I already told her, she can blame me for everything. I don't give a fuck as long as that kid is mine.

She didn't want to find out what the baby's gender was this time around, and I'm fuckin' dying to know, too. The doctor says something about seeing the baby's head, and that she needs to give one more big push. She screams as she pushes one more time, and I hear the unremarkable screams of the baby she just delivered.

Trix starts to pant, and I look over to see a little

baby covered in a filmy residue. Yeah, I'm not big on knowing the technical terms for that shit. I look back at Trix, and she has tears coming from her eyes. The nurse hands me these weird scissor like things, and I look at her with a questioning look. "Would the father like to cut the umbilical cord?" I look over at Trix, and she nods her head tiredly.

"Yeah." My voice is choked up and, when I see the little girl in nurse's arms, I can't help but smile. She's fuckin' perfect just like her mother. She has pale skin and dark hair just like Blade and me. After cutting the umbilical cord, they do a few more things before they bring her over to Trix. When the nurse finally puts her on Trix's chest, I watch in awe. Seeing my girl do that is the best thing in the fuckin' world. I missed the birth of Blade because I was a fuckin' idiot, but I'm glad I got to be here for her birth.

"She's perfect," she whispers, looking up at me with tears in her eyes. I walk back over to her side and move the sweaty red hair of her forehead.

"She is, babe. Perfect, just like her momma." I press my lips to her skin and close my eyes.

"She looks so much like Blade did when he was born." Her finger lightly caresses the little girl's cheek, and I can't help but think that there is no way this little girl belongs to Romeo. He may share the same hair color, but that is it. His skin is tan from the Mexican heritage that runs through him and she just as white as Trix. Pale pink skin that is smooth. There is no way she's not mine.

"She has to be mine," I whisper against her skin. When I pull away, I see the tears fill her eyes.

"You don't know how bad I want that for you, but…" She stops from saying anything else as the nurses continue to do whatever it is that there are doing. They take the baby away to do measurements and shit and we are left alone in the room together.

"I want you to be honest with me, Trixibella." She nods her head and I grab her hand. Sitting in the chair next to her bed, I look down at the ground before I ask the question that has been burning inside of me for months. "Do you love him?"

I watch as she mulls over her answer, and I can see it in her eyes that she does. She doesn't even need to say the words to me because it's written all over her face. "More than me?" She finally looks at me and frowns.

"I'll never love any man more than I love you. The closest competition that you'll ever have is about two and a half feet tall with dark brown hair." I grin at that. A knock at the door brings us back from the serious question I asked her, and we watch as they wheel our little girl in. Yeah, I'm claiming she's mine until I hear otherwise.

The nurse brings her over to Trix, and helps her start the feeding process. I watch in awe, as my girl is a natural at it. "You'll do just fine, Trix. You've had practice." The nurse smiles at her, and then walks out of the room. I spend the next ten minutes just watching them. My phone starts to ring and, when I look down, it's Prez.

"Yeah?" I answer.

"Can I bring your boy up? He wants to meet his little brother or sister, and Ro is on his way." I cringe just at his name. It won't matter how long they are together; it will never fuckin' change.

"Yeah, bring him on up. He has a little sister to meet." I hang up and look over to Trix. "So, what are you naming her?" Her head snaps in my direction and she frowns.

"I haven't even thought of a name." She looks back down at the dark-haired baby, who is now passed out on her mother's chest. "Do you know of anything good?" A smile tips from her lips, and I look back at the little girl.

"Bexley Makena."

"I love it," she whispers. The door opens, and I see Prez walk in with a very excited little boy. Blade runs to me, and he wraps his arms around my arm.

"Hey buddy, you want to meet your sister?" He nods, and I pick him up to sit in my lap. He looks over at his mom and then points a finger at his sister.

"She nakey!" he squeals. Says the kid that loves to run around butt naked himself. I shake my head at him and start to laugh. He reaches over, and runs his hand softly over his sister's dark hair that matches his own. "Wuv momma," he whispers. I stand up and lift him, so he can give his momma a kiss on the lips followed by kissing his sister's head.

When I take a seat back in my chair, Prez walks over to her and presses a kiss to her forehead. He leans in and says something, but I don't catch it. Blade hands me his blanket, and he curls up in my lap. I wrap his blanket around him, and we both watch his momma and sister.

When Prez is done talking to Trix, he comes over to me and puts his hand out. "Do I need to stick around for you two assholes to get along, or are you going to be civil for once?" I reach out and take his hand shaking it.

"Yeah, I'll be cool. But it will only be for today." He smirks at me and I grin. He knows just as well as I do that I don't want to be fuckin' pleasant to that dickhead, but I will for her.

"Trix, call me if they start up with their bitching." She smiles at Prez, and he runs his hand over Blade's hair. "Bye, kid. I'll see you later."

Blade gives him a sleepy wave and I smile. I watch as Prez walks out, and Trix asks if I want to hold her. Looking at the little girl in her arms, I grin and move my chair closer to the bed and lean forward without knocking Blade off my lap. She hands me the little girl, and I see the similarities. She looks like a mix between Blade and Trix. Blade mostly takes after me, but I see his momma in him in the subtlest ways.

When the door opens again, I hear his booted feet hit the ground in heavy steps. I know he hates the fact that he wasn't here when she went into labor and, as much as I want to be the asshole that rubs it in his face, I keep quiet. He walks over to the other side of her bed and gives her a kiss. Blade sits up in my lap, and tries to look at his sister more closely. When Romeo finally gets a good look at the little girl in my arms, I can see the anger cross his features. He knows the answer already, too.

This kid isn't his.

He sits on the bed next to her, watching me. I hold the little girl until she starts to cry. Handing her back to Trix, I see the disgust written all over his face. He probably told her a bunch of lies that they were going to stay together and shit, even if the baby wasn't his, but I have a feeling that they won't last. Hell, I'm banking on that little fact. She's mine, and there is nothing standing in my way of me getting what's mine.

Chapter Six

In the days since the birth of Bexley, I haven't seen much of my Trixibella. She's been distant since I left the room after I helped her through the birth of that precious little girl. *My* little girl. Grabbing my phone, I dial her number and wait for her to answer.

"Hey, E. I was just going to send you a picture." She sounds off, kinda like she's been crying.

"What's wrong, Trixibella?" My voice is growing strained, and she doesn't say anything for the longest time. I hear Blade in the background and the coos of Bexley.

"Nothing. I just…" She trails off for a second before she starts to speak again. "I don't know how I could have messed this up so much." It sounds like she sniffs a few times before she gets her emotions under control.

"You haven't messed up, baby," I reply. I know it's not a good enough answer but, in my eyes, she hasn't. The only thing I would change is that she was back in my arms, not his.

"I sent in the paternity test," she whispers. Her voice breaks, and I know this shit is hard for her. "I know in my heart who her father is, but I wanted the proof on paper, too." I lean my head back against the couch and run my hand over my eyes. I need a fuckin' drink or ten.

"And, who is that?" I ask. I want her to say me so damn bad that I don't even realize that I'm grinding my teeth so hard that my jaw aches.

"You already know the answer to that, E," she says quietly.

"I want to hear you say the words," I say through gritted teeth. When I finally unclench my jaw, I can feel the pain and the tension ease. Fuck, she makes me goddamn crazy.

"You," she chokes out. I hear a door close, and

his voice drift through the damn house.

"Hey babe. You home?" I can imagine her wiping her eyes, and taking a few deep breaths, before she answers him.

"Yeah, I'm in here," she calls out to him. "I'm sorry, E. I'll bring Blade by tomorrow for you." I listen to the line go dead, and the only thing I can think of right now is getting drunk and fuckin' some bitch. I won't even be all that picky; I just need to get her out of my mind.

Checking my contacts, I scroll through until I find one of my buddies and hit the call button. "Hey, fucker," he greets on the third ring.

"Hey, asshole. You want to head with me to the bar?" I ask.

"You know it. It's a sure thing for me to get laid if I show up with your ass." I chuckle and tell him to swing by in a few hours. When I hang up the phone, I lie back on the couch and think about those two little angels that I helped create. Closing my eyes, I think about their mother and how I've fucked things up with her. I told her from the beginning that I was a bastard, and that no woman would change me. I think she took that as a challenge.

Three years ago

Walking into the clubhouse, my eye catches on the beautiful redhead sitting at the bar. Her back is to me and, just judging by the group of brother's around her, she has to be something else. When I finally get closer, I feel like the wind got knocked out of me. I never messed around on my wife before, but the woman before me makes me want to question all my morals. Not saying that I'm a fuckin' angel, because my wife can definitely attest to the bastard that I am.

When her eyes meet mine, she gives me a sly smile and gets to her feet. She walks towards me on these fuck me heels that have my dick standing at attention.

I know I married the wrong fuckin' woman, but this woman standing in front of me has the power to bring me to my knees.

"Hi," she breathes. Her fingers start at my left shoulder and move across to my right. She licks her lips, and

I feel my dick tighten in my jeans. "I'm Trixie." I reach out and grab her hand, pulling her closer to me. Her warm breath fans out on my skin, as she looks up at me in slight shock.

My hand reaches up and runs down the side of her face. Her eyes notice my wedding ring, and she pulls away slightly. I can tell she's nervous about me being married, but she doesn't shy away from me completely. "I'm E," I rasp. I run my nose down her neck, and I hear a few of the brothers behind me yell out a few obscenities, but I just ignore them. Those fuckers are always saying something stupid.

"E," she whispers.

"Easy E, either fuck her or take her to your damn room," one of the brothers says from behind me. I don't even bother to flip him the bird because my full attention is on the woman standing in front of me. I feel like the whole world stopped spinning, and it's just the two of us standing here staring into each other's eyes.

"Come on." I whisper, grabbing her hand. She lets me lead her towards my room. I don't slow until the door is shut behind us and I'm pushing her against the door. Pressing my body against hers, I run my hands down her sides and she looks me in the eyes.

Before I can pick her up, her voice breaks the lust-

fused haze I'm in. "You're married." Her voice is no more than a whisper, and I can see the uncertainty written all over her face.

"I've been married since I was eighteen to a bitch that only wants one thing from me." I run my fingers down the side of her face and she lets out a breathy sigh. "She only wants money and status, and I don't have either. I bought her a nice house, and gave her everything she wanted, and she's still a bitch. That ain't ever gonna change. I've been done with her for a long time." Her body shudders as I run my other hand around her back and up her spine, pulling us even closer together.

Instead of telling me she doesn't want to get involved with me, she presses her lips against mine. An animal instinct takes over, and I devoured her mouth with mine. Nipping and sucking my way down her neck, I come to the top of her tits and I yank the tight tube top down. Her big beautiful breasts spill out of the material, and I pull a nipple between my teeth. Her hands grip the back of my head, and she pushes my mouth where she wants it.

Pulling her tight skirt up, I run my fingers under her lace thong, running my fingers through her wet pussy. Her fuckin' body is goddamn perfect, and I can't wait to sink inside of her. Lifting her up, she wraps her legs around my waist as I work to get my jeans undone. Never has a bitch put me into a damn frenzy the way she is. The only thing I can think of is getting my dick inside of her and claiming her pussy as mine.

I know that I have no right to do it since I'm married, but I don't give a fuck. I want her, only her.

Her moans fill my room, and I line my dick up with her soaking wet cunt. I start to push the head inside of her, and her nails dig into my skin. "Oh, god," she whimpers. I thrust into her the rest of the way, and hear her groan. "E." She moans out my name, and I want her to call me by my given name. Fuck, I don't know why, but I know hearing my name from her lips will fuckin' destroy me.

"Call me Elec," I grunt, as I thrust inside of her harder and faster.

"Elec," she moans. Fuck, just hearing my name come from her lips gets me harder than Tina ever did. "Please fuck me harder, Elec." I grunt out and thrust in and out of her with a frenzied pace until we are both coming together. She screams out and bites on my neck to quiet herself as she falls off the damn edge. Her body shakes, as her orgasm hit her hard, and I feel her sweet cunt squeeze the shit out of my

dick.

I pump my hips a few more times as I ride out my orgasm and bury my face into her neck. Her red hair covers my face, and I can smell her sweet scent as it envelops us both. God. What I wouldn't do to get inside of her cunt every fuckin' day.

When I catch my damn breath, I press my mouth to hers and claim it. I want to own her: every damn inch of her body, mind, and soul. I want it to be mine and only mine. Walking us towards the bed, I lay us both down, but don't separate our bodies. I roll us over so she is lying on top of me and she sits up and straddles me, not letting us separate either.

"Elec," she whispers, lifting my shirt up so she can see all that I have underneath. She starts tracing one of the tattoos that cover half of my chest. Her fingers trace the flowers, and then the skulls one by one, and I watch a grin spread across her face. "So, Mr. Married Man, do you have any kids that you go home to at night?" I grin at her and shake my head no.

"Nope. I didn't want to procreate with the bitch I'm married to, so I took care of that shit a long time ago." She frowns at me, and I put my fingers into a scissor like motion

and act like I'm snipping. Her nose wrinkles, and she looks down towards where we are connected.

"So, what happens if you want kids?" she asks. Her fingers start to move again on my skin, and I shrug my shoulders.

"Never thought about kids with the life I lead. I'm not fit to be a father, and there is no fuckin' way that I'd give the chance to Tina to be a mother. She's like a fuckin' cancer. She destroys you from the inside out." Her eyes widen and I run my hands up her sides, catching on her damn skirt and top. Pulling her down on me, I grab the bottom of her top and pull it up and over her head.

"When did you get that done?" she asks curiously.

"A few months after I got married. I always bagged it before then, and, hell, I still did until I stopped fuckin' the crazy bitch a few months ago."

"So, you don't have sex with her anymore?" Her question is barely audible.

"Haven't in months," I reply. I roll her back over, and let her take my shirt off. She tosses it on the ground behind me and uses her feet to start to work my jeans down my thighs and to my feet. Kicking the jeans and my boots off, I feel my dick start to get ready again. She wiggles a little,

and I groan at the sensations. Her body fuckin' sets mine off likes it's a damn wildfire and we're going to burn the damn place up.

I roll her back over to straddle me as I grip her skirt and start to slide the tight materials up her body until I get it off of her. Her giggles fill the air and when I finally pull it over her head, she pulls me up into a sitting position. She presses her tits into my face and I grab her panties and give them a hard yank. She gasps as the material falls away from her body and I just grin.

"So, Trixie, is that you're real name or just a nickname?" She giggles and brings her mouth down to mine. Her tongue slips between my lips, and I let her set the pace. I hear my phone ring in my jeans, but there is no fuckin' way I'm leaving her sweet cunt tonight. I'm staying buried inside of her until she can't walk, and I'm the only man she can feel between her thighs for weeks to come.

"Trixibella. But if you tell anyone my real name, I'll kill you." She gives me her meanest look, and I just grin at her. She's fuckin' cute as all hell, trying to threaten me.

"Well, I'd say the same for you. I don't go by Elec normally. Its pronounced Elec as in election. Don't ask why my parents named me that. Either people can't fuckin' say

the damn name or they talk shit for how different it is." She frowns at my words, and runs a finger between my eyes, smoothing the wrinkles that I'm sure are on my face from the memories of everyone taking shit about my name.

"I can call you Elec?" Her eyes are full of humor, and she leans us both down on the mattress.

"You can call me whatever you want," I murmur before taking her again.

Chapter Seven

I spend the rest of my night out with my boy Tarak. He isn't a fuckin' biker, and he can pull more ass than most fuckin' men. He thinks I'm the reason he gets lucky. Really, that cocksucker is full of shit. If anything, it's his ass that is bringing all the bitches to us. He rides, but refuses to join the Draconic Crimson MC. Trust me, I fuckin' tried for months to no avail.

Making our way to the bar, I see a pair of twins that keep eye-fuckin' the shit out of us. I smack the fucker on the back, nod in the direction of the girls, and he leads the mother fuckin' way. When we get up to them, the first one practically eye fucks the asshole while the other starts to make her way towards me. Her dark hair does nothing for me, but that's just because

I'm hung up on what I can't fuckin' have right now. She pushes out her small tits and rubs up against me.

"Buy me a drink?" She bats her eyelashes at me and I nod my head. Turning to the bar, I motion for the bartender and, when she sees my cut, she practically runs over to me.

"What can I get for you, stud?" she purrs. The bitch next to me comes to stand in front of me, and turns to face me.

"I'll take a vodka cranberry." She bats her eyelashes at me some more, and I look over her at the bartender and order three shots of Jack for me and three for Tarak. I order the girls both a cran-whatever and hand the bitch behind the bar some cash. When she hands me my change, I see the paper with her number on it. I wink at her and hand the shots to Tarak and the drink to the bitch he's with. We make our way towards a table, and I set the shots down and instantly take one.

I feel my phone vibrate and, when I pull it out of my pocket, I see Trix's name across the screen. Hitting the open button, I see a picture of Blade holding his sister. The picture tears at my damn black heart, and I want nothing more than to be there instead of this shitty ass bar.

I feel Tarak looking over my shoulder and he hits it with his. "You have another one?" he asks. I nod, but I don't say anything. The bitch comes over and checks out the picture on my phone and then practically dry humps me. Fuck, I need more alcohol for this shit.

"Those you're nephews?" she asks in an annoying ass whiny tone. I don't get why some bitches sound whiny all the damn time. Whatever fuckin' happened to the ones with the sexy rasps that head straight to your dick? My mind thinks back to Trix and my kids.

"No, that's my son and my daughter," I grit out. Grabbing the last two shots, I down them quickly and make my way back to the bar. Fuck, I need way more than this shit. I order some more shots and some asshole comes up to me with something he says is a little stronger. I watch him for a second, and then look back at the table. The girls are dancing with each other, I know that they don't need shit, and I tell him to get fuckin' lost.

I don't want to do shit to ruin my chance with Trix and I know that if she finds out about me doing drugs of any sort, she will pack my kids up and get the fuck out of town. Her mother was a druggie, and that was the one thing she made me promise her that I would never do, especially after she got pregnant.

When I get the drinks and pay for them, I make my way back to the table and set one of the glasses down, just as the bitch that was all over me wraps her hand around my neck, and pulls me to her body. I down another shot, and set the empty glass back on the table.

She runs her hand down my chest and to the top of my jeans. My phone beeps again with another message, so I pull it out of my pocket and check the screen. I see Prez's name on my screen, and I hit the button to open the message.

Prez: ***Got a run for you. You'll be out of town for a few weeks. You game?***

I run my hand over my face and the bitch slides her hand into my jeans, gripping my dick in her palm.

My mind instantly thinks about Trix and how she would do the same fuckin' shit when I wasn't paying attention to her. My dick stiffens in the bitch's hand, and she looks up at me and grins.

Me: ***Yeah. I got you Prez.***

Prez: ***Good. I got the details on the desk at the club. Come by and get them when you get a minute.***

Me: ***I'll be by tomorrow.***

Instead of putting my phone back in my pocket like I should, I send Trix a message back.

Me: ***Love the photo. Do I get both kids tomorrow?***

When she doesn't respond right away, I finally tuck my phone in my pocket and turn my attention to the bitch whose hand is steadily jerking me off in the crowded bar. I let her work me up for a few more minutes before I wrap my arm around her and pull her closer to my body. Leaning down to her ear, I whisper, "You want me to fuck you?" Her eyes shoot to mine, and she nods eagerly. I motion my head towards the back, and lead her past Tarak and her sister. I slap him on the shoulder as we pass, and motion to the direction we were heading. He nods and makes his way with us, the other bitch trailing behind him like a little fuckin' puppy.

When we get to the back of the bar, I push the bitch into the dark corner and face her. Her eyes brighten at the thought of getting my dick and I force her to her knees. As much as I need to get off, I don't really want to fuck her.

She undoes my jeans, and I watch as she slowly pulls me out. Looking over at Tarak, I see him push the other bitch against the wall with his hand up her short as fuck skirt. The bitch on her knees strokes me a few times and I close my eyes. Pretending she's Trix is the only way I can even get it fuckin' up right now. Goddamn that woman; she fuckin' owns me.

My dick gets harder with each thought of my girl, and the bitch sucks me like she can't get fuckin' enough. Her nails lightly scratch my dick, and I shoot off into her mouth. She cleans me up with some fuckin' suction that doesn't really compare, and I pull her up to my mouth. Before I press my mouth to hers, I pull back.

I started to get lost in the thought that I had Trix sucking my dick. Fuck. The bitch frowns, and I pull her closer to me. I nip and suck at her neck to make up for pulling away and lift her up and press her against the wall. Her legs wrap around me and I slide her flimsy panties to the side. Grabbing a condom out of my back pocket, I slip it on and slowly slide into the bitch's pussy. Her nails dig into my shoulders and she moans out.

If the music wasn't so fuckin' loud, the whole damn place would hear the way this bitch screams. I fuck her hard and fast, making sure she comes before I finish. Pulling out of her quickly, I let her slide down my body and she kisses all down my neck. She fixes her skirt and I tuck myself back into my jeans.

"Let's head back to your place," Tarak suggests. The girls both eagerly nod their heads, and I shrug. At least at the house, I can get fuckin' shit faced and not worry about being able to get it up later.

The blankets are being pulled off my body and I groan at the light. Just before I pull the blanket back down on me, I feel the fuckin' cold ass water being poured on me. Leaping out of my damn bed, I whirl around to see Trix standing there with her hand on her hip and the water pitcher in her hand. "Get the whore out of here," she demands. The bitch screams as Trix pours water onto her next.

"You stupid bitch," the chick from last night screeches. She makes her way towards Trix, but I grab her and pull her back.

"Don't even fuckin' think about touching her," I growl. The bitch from last night changes her damn tone quickly, and wraps an arm around me. "You heard her. Get the fuck out." She frowns, releasing me, before she gives Trix the evil eye. We both watch as she gathers her shit quickly, and makes her way towards the master bathroom.

"Real fucking classy, E. I guess you're just living up to your nickname finally," she spits. I make my way over to her, and she backs up until I trap her against the wall.

I put my hands on either side of her and her eyes meet mine. "I had to think about you just to get fuckin' hard last night. And, while I was fuckin' her, it was you that I was picturing under me. You've fuckin' ruined me baby. Call that fuckin' idiot up and tell him it's over. I want my family." I hear her sharp gasp and she pushes against my chest, trying to get free from the wall.

"Elec," she whispers. She shakes her head no and looks towards the ground as the bathroom door opens. I don't let her leave and we both watch as the bitch leaves the room, slamming the door behind her. She must have heard what I told Trix.

"Trixibella, there is no one else is this fuckin' world for me. You are fuckin' it, and I am tired of letting that fuckin' bastard come between us. We have two fuckin' beautiful kids together, and we deserve to give this shit a real damn shot." Her eyes brighten and then I watch as they fill with tears. She doesn't say a word, and I know I've already lost the war over her heart.

Leaning forward, I claim her mouth in a slow

kiss. Her hands go to my chest and move around to my back as she pulls me closer to her. Our bodies are fuckin' made for each other, and I wish like fuckin' hell that she would just give me a second chance.

When I break our kiss, I press my forehead against hers and blow out a breath. My dick is pressed up against her body, and I know she can feel how damn hard I am for her. "I love you, Trixibella." I press one more kiss to her forehead before I hear our terror screaming in the other room. Releasing her, I walk towards my dresser and pull on a pair of jeans. I don't even bother putting a shirt on as I walk back over to her.

The frown never leaves her face, and I pull her back into my arms. "What's wrong?" I ask. I move a strand of hair out of her face, and she wraps her arms around me, squeezing me tightly.

"How the hell do we always end up here? All I've wanted since the day I met you was to be yours. Nothing else mattered. We were supposed to beat the odds. I knew that I was always going to have to share a part of you with her, and part of me didn't mind, as long as I had the part of you that mattered." She puts her hand over my heart and closes her eyes.

I feel her deeply breathe, and when she opens her eyes again, I see the regret and pain that I cause. "I'll always love you, Elec. There is no one else that fits me better than you. You gave me Blade and Bexley. There is nothing that can change that and, at the end of the day, I know that if I needed you, you're just a phone call away. You pick me up when I need it, and you'll always be the man I need more than my next breath."

She wipes the tears from under her eyes before she gets on her tiptoes and kisses me. She turns to walk out the door, but I catch her wrist and pull her back into me. "You're under my skin. We may hate each other at times, but the love never dies. I don't want it to. I want to have you in my arms every fuckin' night and every damn day. We fight, we make up. It's what we fuckin' do, baby girl. It will never change, but it is us."

She nods her head and I grab her chin, pulling her mouth to mine one last time. I release her, and we walk into the living room where I see my boy climbing all over Tarak who looks like he has a hangover. I walk over to the car seat that is sitting by the couch and I kneel down to look at my sleeping angel. Running the tip of my finger over her soft cheek, I feel her eyes on me. When I look behind me, I see the look on Trix's face. It's a mix of love and heartbreak.

After pressing a soft kiss to Bex's head, I watch Trix walk over to us, grabbing the car seat. "I'll walk you out," I say before she can walk away from me. I grab the car seat out of her hand, and she walks over to grab Blade and give him a kiss.

"I love you, baby," she says to him. He leans over to her on the edge of the couch and kisses her on the mouth.

"Wuv you, momma!" he says excitedly. He goes back to jumping on Tarak, and I can see her body sag. I know that she hates leaving him here with me. Same way I feel when I have to give him back to her at the end of my time with him.

She leads me to the door and opens it, looking back at our boy as him and Tarak wrestle. "He'll be fine, babe," I whisper in her ear. Her body breaks out in a shiver, and she looks at me over her shoulder.

"I know. I just hate when he's away from me." She blows out a breath before continuing. "It's going to be worse when I have to leave both of them here and I walk out that door." My chest comes up against her back and she melts against me.

"You know there is a way around that." I kiss right below her ear in the place that gets her every time. She nods her head, but doesn't say another word to me. When we finally get to her car, I strap the car seat in, and stare at my little girl for a moment before I shut the door. Trix is standing by her door, looking at the ground, when I pull my attention from Bexley.

Before I can even see if anything is wrong with Trix, she walks over to me and wraps her arms around my neck. She hugs me close to her body and I am shocked. My arms wrap around her automatically and I breathe in her scent, memorizing it. Who the fuck knows the next time I'm going to get to have her in my arms like this again?

We stand like this for what seems like hours, but

I know it's only a few minutes. Her phone starts to ring, and she pulls away from me. Watching as she pulls it from her purse, I see his name on the screen. "Hey," she answers, wiping at one of her eyes. "Yeah, I'll be on my way back in a few minutes." She pauses and looks up at me. The frown on her face doesn't give me any insight into how she feels about this shit that is still between us.

"Okay. I…" She pauses and looks up at me as she stops herself from saying the words. "I'll see you soon. Bye." Closing my eyes, I feel the anger eat me up on the inside. She was going to tell him that she loved him. *Fuck.* I rub absently at my heart, and her eyes watch me the whole time. "E," she whispers, breaking me from my trance.

"Yeah?" I ask, looking up, still rubbing right over my heart.

"The test results come in tomorrow. Do you want me to call you with the results?" I shake my head no and I watch as her face falls.

"I want you to come here when you get them. I want them in person." Her eyes widen slightly before a small grin appears on her face.

"Okay." She comes closer to me, and gives me a small peck on my cheek, before getting into the car and driving away with the other piece of my barely beating heart.

Chapter Eight

Spending the rest of my night with my boy made my day fuckin' worth every minute. Before bed, he wanted to call his sister and say goodnight. Grabbing my phone off the table, I put the Facetime app on and hit Trix's number. Blade doesn't go to bed without saying goodnight to his momma.

I see her face appear on the screen, and her wipe her eyes. "Hey, baby." She smiles at him. She looks at me and gives me a slight shake to keep me from saying shit.

"Momma!" Blade squeaks out. I watch him give her kissy faces on the phone, and all you see is his big head filling the entire screen.

"Hey, baby. Are you having a good time with

daddy?" she asks him. He nods his head a bunch of times like a damn bobble head. He sits back in my lap, and I hold the phone out for him to see her better. "Did you guys do anything fun?" Her voice is low and she sounds upset.

"We payed at park!" he says excitedly.

"Oh yeah?" she asks. He nods his head and then gets off my lap to go and find his new toy he got today. We spent an hour at the damn toy store looking for the damn thing that he said he had to have.

"What's wrong?" I ask. She shakes her head no, and I push the subject more. "Just fuckin' tell me," I demand. She gives me a dirty look before she sighs and looks around the room.

"I got the results early," she whispers. I swallow the lump in my throat. I try to say something to her, but I can't get anything out.

"And?" I finally get the word out. It wasn't what I wanted to fuckin' ask, but it was the only word I could push past my lips. I watch her breath shutter, and she looks away from the screen for a second, before she turns her light eyes back to me.

"He isn't talking to me. Romeo is pissed at the results. I'm pretty sure he hates the fact that you are their father."

Blowing out the breath I didn't even realize I was holding, I run a hand over my face. "Thank fuck," I whisper just as Blade comes back into the room holding his new toy. He climbs back into my lap and looks at the screen to see his momma crying.

"Momma? No sad?" His lip trembles as he watches his momma cry, and it breaks my heart.

"I'm okay, baby. I'm just happy. Okay?" He watches her for a second before he nods his head. "What is that?" she finally asks, breaking his concentration on her face.

"Daddy bawft me dis!" He holds his new laptop-like fuckin' thing up and shows her what it does for about ten minutes before he asks where his sister is. Trix picks Bexley up and cradles her in her arms. "Sissy," he says with a big smile. He grabs the phone and pulls it to his face to do his kissy face again.

He talks to her some more and I pull him back against my chest. We watch her yawn and stretch a few times before she starts to cry. "I need to feed her," Trix says.

Before I tell her that's fine, Blade tells her that he doesn't want them to go yet. I tell her that I'm fine with her feeding in front of me. She looks at me hesitantly, and then back down at our daughter, who's screaming her head off. "It's not like I haven't seen you naked a thousand times," I grin. She gives me the finger and then pulls her tit out and starts to feed Bex.

Just watching her feed our daughter makes my heart constrict. Fuck, I want her back. I was a fuckin' idiot to make her promises that I continued to break. She's what I should have been fighting for, instead of just not giving a fuck about anything but myself.

Blade continues to talk her ear off and I just watch her. I watch the way she cuddles our daughter, running her finger down Bex's face and then continues to stroke her dark hair out of her eyes. I don't remember Blade ever having as much hair as Bexley.

I move Blade off the center of my lap, and I have to adjust myself without letting her know that she's getting me hard just sitting there feeding our daughter.

God, I could watch her all damn day. *Shit*. I've spent mornings worshipping that body of hers, and nights tangled up in the sheets with her fuckin' her, until we both couldn't move.

A knock at the door brings her head up from our daughter, and she looks at me with a questioning expression. I shrug and set Blade on the couch and hand him the phone. Walking towards the front door, I adjust myself and open the door to see a cop standing there. "Hi, are you Elec Briody?" he says. His eyes scan over me, and I lean against the door jam.

"Why?" I ask. I hear Blade talking to Trix still, and the cop tries to look around me and inside.

"Do you know a Tina Briody?" he asks after looking at a pad of paper.

"She's my ex-wife." I raise an eyebrow and I can only imagine the shit she's going to try and pull now that she's no longer married to me. She vowed to make my life hell when I signed the divorce papers, and I guess she's finally going to make good on her threat. "What did she say this time? That I'm abusing my son? That bitch needs to get a damn life." I watch him and he looks uneasy.

"You have a child together?" he asks with a raised eyebrow.

"No," I say, shaking my head. "I have a son with someone else and she's pissed about it." He writes down a few things before he raises his head and looks at me with remorse. What the fuck is goin'… *Fuck.* Everything clicks. Something happened to her.

"I'm sorry to inform you, Mr. Briody, but Mrs. Briody was found murdered last night." I drop my head, and I hear Blade's little feet slamming against the hardwood floor as he comes towards the door. He grabs it and pulls it open, looking up at me.

"Dadda, momma tav ew." He hands me my phone, and I see the unease written all over her face.

"Babe, I need to call you back," I say. Her eyebrows furrow and she goes to say something, but I look up at the cop who doesn't bother to even look like he isn't listening. When I look back at the screen, she nods her head and hangs up without another word. Pocketing my phone, I pick up Blade and hold him to me.

"So, Mr. Briody, where were you last night?" He starts to write notes, and I want to laugh at his pansy ass.

"I was at a bar with my buddy and I had some bitch blow me in the back. After that, we brought them back here and let's just say I had her screaming my name all night long." He looks at Blade and then back at me.

"And, who was watching your son?" His tone isn't something I like and I need to protect her, too.

"His mother had him and his sister last night," I state. He takes a step back from me and looks me in the eyes.

"Could she have left them with someone else when she went to kill your wife?" Putting Blade down, I tell him to go inside and play with his new toy. He runs inside, and I shut the door behind me.

Getting right in the cops face, I point my finger at his chest. "She didn't give a fuck about my ex-wife. We have a two-week-old daughter. She doesn't have time to shower in the morning, much less leave the damn house. Leave her the fuck alone. I don't know what happened to Tina, but you can bet your ass she fuckin' deserved it."

He eyes me for a second before he grins. "Don't worry, I'll find out who murdered your ex-wife, and I'll make sure that they are charged to the fullest extent of the law. You have a good day. I suggest you find a nanny if your baby momma winds up in jail."

Fuck. As much as I want to go after that fuckin' cop, I stand my ground. He gives me one last smirk before he turns and walks back towards his unmarked car. Grabbing my phone out of my pocket, I dial Trix's number. When she finally answers, I can't get the words out fast enough.

"Where were you last night?" I bark out, making my way into the house. I look over at Blade and see him passed out on the couch already. Not giving him a nap worked wonders tonight.

"What the hell are you talking about? I was at home with the kids," she says, sounding pissed off at me for even asking.

"Tina is dead. They think we had something to do with it. I just had a cop at my door asking where I was last night and where you were." I hear her suck in a breath over the line and I pace the living room. "Trix, tell me you didn't," I whisper. She wouldn't have done that. I know her better than that.

"Seriously? You have to ask me that, E? You know me better than that," she huffs out.

"I know baby, but this shit is serious. I have a feeling he is going to go to your place and question you." Running my hand over my face, I hate asking this damn question. "Was he with you last night?" She gets quiet, and the only sound I can hear is my own heart beating fast. My adrenaline is spiking and I need to do something, anything. Even if it were her, I wouldn't let her go down for the murder of Tina.

"No. I told you we had a fight and he isn't really talking to me." She sounds like she's about to cry.

"Come over here. Get you and Bexley in the car and drive straight here."

"Won't that cop know who I am?"

"No. I don't think he knows your name. He will probably be searching my phone records to find your info. Just get here now, and I'll figure something out. I won't let anyone pin this shit on you." I look at our son and then tell her, "I love you."

"I'm scared." Her voice breaks, and I know she's probably freaking out right now.

"I know, babe. Just get here and I'll protect you," I state. She tells me she's on her way and I wait for her to hang up. Once I get her here, I'll at least be able to protect her.

Dialing Prez's number, I wait for him to pick up. "Come on," I mutter to myself. When he finally picks up, I can hear the frustration in his voice.

"What, E? I'm already dealing with enough shit and you pissing off my VP doesn't make that shit any easier," he whispers something to someone before he gets back on the phone.

"Tina is dead," I say with no emotion.

"What?" He bites out. "What the fuck do you mean she's dead?"

"Exactly what I fuckin' said. I just had a damn cop at my door asking where I was last night. He was asking about Trix, too."

"Fuck. They think she did it?" he asks. "Hey

prospect, find me Romeo now!" He yells out.

"I don't know. She's coming to me right now. I'll bring her and the kids to the clubhouse," I state. I hear Romeo's voice in the background as Stavros gives him a rundown of what I just said.

"Where is she?" he asks. Stavros tells him that she's on her way to me, and I can hear him curse. "Of course, she fucking runs to him," he says under his breath, but loud enough for me to hear over the line. I swear I want to kill that fucker for even touching her.

My doorbell sounds and I walk towards it to open it, but it opens before I get there. I see the car seat before I see her. When she gets through the door, I feel like I can breathe again. Being worried about her getting hauled in isn't what should be happening. She doesn't deserve that shit.

"Trixibella," I say, grabbing the car seat from her. She drops a bag next to our feet and shuts the door.

"She there?" Stavros asks.

"Yeah, just got here. What's the plan?" I ask, looking her over. She looks like she is on the verge of tears and I hate that. Setting the car seat down on the ground, I reach out a hand, wrapping it around the back of her neck and pulling her body to mine. I don't care if she gets pissed about me touching her; I need to feel her body right now.

I feel her sharp intake of breath, and her hands grip my back, holding me to her. "Bring them here and we will start figuring out a plan," he says sternly.

"Be there soon," I say curtly before I hang up. Putting my phone in my pocket, I wrap my other arm around her and hold her. "I'll take the fall before I let anything happen to you," I whisper against the side of her head.

Her eyes snap up to mine and I can see the tears forming. "No. I won't let you do that," she says adamantly.

"I won't let you go down for it, babe. They need you more than me." I kiss her forehead and I hear our holy terror as he starts to wake back up.

Chapter Nine

When I get them all to the clubhouse, Stavros and Romeo are standing in the lot watching us pull in. Grabbing a sleeping Blade out of the back seat of my Chevy, I prop his face against my shoulder and shut the door. Walking over to Trix's side, I grab the car seat from her, and lead her towards Stavros and her douche bag boyfriend.

She doesn't go towards him, and part of me gets fuckin' excited about that. It means I still have a chance to get her back. She stays close to me as we come to a stop in front of them. "Hey Trixi," Stavros says. She gives him a smile, but doesn't say anything.

I can feel the anger radiating off of Romeo, but he doesn't say a word. He's never been known to fly off the handle, and I know he doesn't like to cause a scene. "I want to get Blade put back into bed," I finally say, breaking some of the tension. Stavros nods and motions for me to leave. When Trix tries to follow me, he steps in her way and stops her.

I knew he wanted to ask her questions and I should have known that he would wait until he got us separated.

"I'll be right back." She hands me the bag and the baby monitor.

"Can you please put this in the room so I know when they wake up?" I nod and she puts the monitor in the car seat and I grab the bag with same hand that has the car seat.

"Your old room is still free, Easy E," Stavros says over his shoulder. I look back at them and I see Romeo's eyes on me. His eyes bore into me, but I don't let it affect me. I'm playing for keeps, and I won't let him win.

After I get Blade settled into my old bed, and put the baby monitor on the table next to it, I look down into the car seat at my daughter. Shit. I never thought that I would be a father, but now that they are here, I wouldn't change that shit for the world. I had sworn that I'd never get a bitch pregnant, and that's why I got fixed so damn young.

I didn't want to live my life by the rules of a child. I love living free, and leaving on the drop of a dime. Hell, half the time I don't even know if I'll be making it home after a run. We've had too many close calls to count.

I knew going through with getting a vasectomy that it could reverse itself, but I never actually expected it to. Plus, I still wore condoms every time I fucked. Well, until Trix. Having her pussy take me in bare was the best damn feeling in the world, and I wanted it every chance I got, so I said fuck it and went bareback.

I don't regret a damn thing. I have two beautiful children by the one woman that I will love the rest of my life. Damn, I sound like such a bitch right now. Kissing both my kids once more, I get up from the bed and make my way back towards where I left them. I can hear Stavros's voice through the clubhouse doors and he sounds fuckin' heated.

Quickly making my towards them, I see the tears streaming down her face. "What the fuck are you thinking, Trix? You're letting him ruin your damn life still." This time, it's Romeo's voice I hear. Her eyes meet mine, and she slightly shakes her head at me to keep me from saying anything. I know she can handle herself, but she shouldn't have to.

When they both turn towards me, I my eyes narrow on Romeo. Before I can stop myself, I grab him by the throat and clock him in the side of the head. Stavros pulls me back before I can swing again. "I didn't fuckin' ruin her life. She fuckin' chose me. You still jealous that Bexley is mine? You want what I have? Go fuck yourself!" I yell at him. Stavros has his hand on my chest, and he's still pushing me back. "I already told you from day one that I wasn't stepping back. She's mine. Those kids in there are mine. You want to take them? You better be ready for one hell of a fight."

Romeo spits blood on the ground and slowly wipes at his mouth. "You being their father doesn't mean shit. I've been the one there for Trix, Blade and Bexley every damn night."

"What, like you were tonight? Where the fuck were you? You want to be her old man? Then you should have been the one to calm her down. She might be arrested for murder because she doesn't have a damn alibi. One that you should be able to provide, but you were fuckin' pissy because Bex isn't yours." I push Stavros to go at him again, but he forces me to stop.

"You want to protect her, then stop. I won't have you throwing out insults to my VP. Just because you went nomad doesn't mean you can mouth off to my men," he says, low enough that only I can hear.

I push away from him again, and, this time, he lets me go. I walk over to Trix, and she climbs into my arms. Pulling her to my body, I look over at Romeo and see the look on his face. He doesn't say anything this time, but I know that it's fuckin' killing him to see her in my arms.

The baby monitor in my pocket goes off with cries from Bex, and I feel her whole body tense. "Come on. She's probably hungry," I whisper against her hair. She looks up at me and nods her head. I lead her away from both Stavros and Romeo. When we get to the door, I can hear Romeo talking shit. He is fuckin' lucky Stavros stopped me.

Getting into the room, I watch as Trix goes to Bex and picks her up. She rocks her and tries to soothe her. I move some boxes off the chair in the corner of the room, and lead them both over to it. Watching Trix take a seat, I see the love in her eyes as she looks down at our little girl.

Her eyes cut to me as I watch her. "She hungry?" I ask. She nods her head and I watch her as she pulls her tit out and starts to feed her. This time, she doesn't have any shame in me seeing her. I hear Blade start to stir, so I make my way over to the bed and take a seat next to his small body. He cuddles into my side, and wraps his little arm around my thigh.

"E," Trix whispers from her spot across the room. My eyes meet hers, and I watch her face. "I'm sorry." She looks back down at Bexley, and moves the hair out of her face.

"Sorry for what?" I ask. My eyes bore into her as I watch her struggle with finding the words. Her eyes scan over Blade, and then run up my body until her eyes stop on my face.

"I'm sorry for everything. You always seem to be cleaning up messes because of me. I didn't kill her and I wouldn't. She may have made my life hell when she found out about Blade, but having him and Bexley make all the shit we went through worth the trouble." Her hand reaches up, and she wipes a tear from her eye.

I look down at Blade, and brush his dark hair off his forehead. "I won't let anything happen to you, babe." I see her eyes on me still, and the sounds of Bexley nursing fill the room. A knock at the door brings my attention away from her and towards it. The door slowly opens, and I see Romeo walk inside. Closing my eyes, I lean my head back against the wall.

As much as I want to beat the fuck out of him for even being in here, he is still her boyfriend. That shit isn't going to change until she says the words, the words that I crave to hear from her sweet lips, the ones that say she chooses me.

"Hey, I need to talk to you," he says to her. His eyes meet mine, but they quickly move back to her. She rolls her eyes at him, and I can't help but laugh.

"What?" she finally says when he doesn't move. "You want to tell me sorry for walking out when I told you the results? Sorry that I haven't been able to get a hold of you all night?" She shakes her head, and turns her attention back to Bexley.

"Can you give us some privacy?" Romeo snaps at me. Like hell I'm leaving him alone with her and the kids.

"No. It's my room for the night, so looks like you're stuck with me while you're in here." I smirk at him and he gives me a dirty look.

"You're such a fuckin' dick," he mutters. He closes the door and walks towards Trix. "Baby, we need to talk about earlier," he starts.

Before he can continue, she stops him. "What could you possibly want to talk about? You walked out on me when I gave you the results of the test. You were so mad that you left without saying a word. Now, you want to come and try to tell me you're sorry? If that is going to be the way you react every damn time something happens, then I can't do this. I need to provide them with the best environment I can and that won't work." She looks over at me, and I watch her.

I know part of her little speech is directed towards me, too. "You mean you just want to fuck him whenever you feel like it." Getting out from Blade's grasp, I get off the bed and walk towards them. Before I can say anything, she puts her hand up.

"It isn't about him. Well part of it is, but not in the way you think, Romeo. Do I love him? Yes. He is the father of my children. That will never change, but he also broke my heart. I can't just forgive that." Her words stop my train of thought. All I can focus on is the shit I've done to her over the years: the fights we've had and the makeup sex that always came after. We fight and fuck more than anything else. It's almost like it's what brings us closer.

"I fell for you, Romeo. You are the exact opposite of Elec, and that's what I love about you. But, walking out when I gave you the results was something he would do. It's the exact thing he did when I told him I was pregnant with Blade. Well, the only difference is we would fight about it. After he walked out, he came back to see me and we had it out. At least when we are fighting, I know he cares." I watch the tears run down her cheeks. Her eyes meet mine and, for the first time, I feel like the biggest bastard.

"He cares enough to fight with me over stupid things that mean something to him. You either let me do what I want or you just walk away." He moves from his spot and walks closer to her. He leans down and presses his mouth to hers. I want to pull him away from her, but I stand my ground and wait it out.

When he pulls away from her, he doesn't say anything until he reaches me. "The cops are outside. They want to talk to her." He walks towards the door, and I follow him. She calls my name before I can walk out the door.

"No. Stay here. Don't leave this room. I'll deal with it." My voice is harsher than I mean for it to be. She frowns at me, and looks down at Bex, so I slip out quickly.

Making my way towards the parking lot, I see Stavros talking to the cops and Romeo stops at his side. He whispers something in his ear, and Stavros turns to look at me. When I stop next to them, I see the cops eyeing me. "Elec Briody," the cop says. "How the fuck did I know I'd find you here?"

The last time I saw this fucker, he carted my ass off to jail for a weapons charge on a run I did. "You already know that I'm part of this club," I quip. "Thinking about donuts clouding your brain again?" He smirks at me, and then looks over my shoulder.

"Miss Trixibella Rawlins." Shit. I told her to stay the fuck in the room. The cop starts to walk towards her, but I step in front of him. "I suggest you step out of the way, Mr. Briody," he says, looking up at me. I've got a few inches on the bastard, and I would love to show him exactly what it means to go after my girl.

"She didn't do it," I spit. He rolls his eyes at me, and goes to walk around me. Her hands land on my lower back and, when I look over my shoulder at her, she has a look do determination written all over her face.

"Oh, yeah, then who did?" He asks looking right at her.

"I did," I state calmly. The cop frowns and looks

at me. "And I want a lawyer." I hear Trix gasp behind me, and Stavros swears under his breath. The cop then turns me around, and I can see the devastation written all over her face. She shakes her head like she going to say something, but, when she sees the expression on my face, she stops.

I feel the cuffs being placed on my wrists, and the fucker tightens them as roughly as he can. "You have the right to remain silent. Anything you say can and will be used against you in the court of law…" He keeps going, but my focus is solely on her and only her.

"Fuckin' hell," Stavros says. "I'll call our lawyers and have them meet you at the station." As the cop pulls me away from her, I hear her voice.

"Stav, do something!" she yells at him. "Please, you can't let him go to prison." Her cries get muffled and, when I look back, I see him holding her to his body. Her hands are gripping his arms, and I watch as Romeo turns to her and whispers something in her ear. As the cop puts me into the back of the car, I see him pull her into him. When he looks up at me, I can see the satisfaction written all over his face.

If this is part of his plan to win her over, I'll make sure he goes down with me.

Chapter Ten

After they brought me in, they threw me in an interrogation room. I've been in this fuckin' room for the last three hours. When the door finally opens, I see one of our lawyers come walking in the room. She's the girl I've known most of my life, and the same one that I had when I went down for the gun charges. "Elec, I thought we decided you weren't going down again?" She gives me a grin, and I can't help but smirk.

"What can I say, Mica? I was dying to see you again."

"Oh, please. I know for a fact that isn't the truth. I hear you're a father now. Congratulations. Never thought I'd see the day." She sets her briefcase down, and pulls out a notepad and a pen. "So, why don't you tell me what happened and I'll get you out of here?"

"They think my baby momma killed my ex-wife." I don't say anything else because I'm sure those stupid fuckin' cops are listening in. They are about as crooked as the damn politicians in this town. They will do anything for a buck, and I already know I have a price on my head in Ireland. It's the reason I never went back home.

"Are you protecting her?" I don't say anything, but I reach for her pad of paper and pen. I write out one word. Yes.

"Elec..." she starts, but stops when she sees the look on my face. I don't give a fuck what anyone else says. I'll take the jail sentence over seeing her in a place like this. "Please be aware of what you are doing. I've known you a long time, and I don't want to see you wind up in here. Do you have any proof that clears your name?" The pointed look she's giving me means that she is talking about Trix, too.

"No. Nothing that will stand up in court. I need you to get a message out to Stavros and my girl."

"Okay," she says hesitantly. I start to write out a

note for Stavros on the pad of paper and then write one to Trix.

Trixibella,

I know you're probably pissed at me right now, but I did what I had to. I told you I'd protect you, and I would do it over and over again. I love you and our kids more than anything in the world, and I will always protect the three of you. Keep your head up, baby. Shit will get better. Tell my boy that I love him and I'll see him soon. Give my little girl a kiss for me.

-E

After writing one out to Stavros, I hand Mica both the letters, and there is a knock on the door. She tucks the papers into her briefcase before she gets up and walks to the door. "Miss Duncan," one of the cops greets her.

"Hello, Marcus," she says, sweetly. I lean back in my chair, and watch as her ass sways back towards me. The cop clears his throat as he takes a seat, and I can only imagine that he's staring at her ass like I was. The only thing that has ever kept me from fuckin' Mica was that she's my best friend's little sister. I grew up with her and I could never cross that line, no matter how hot she got.

"Let's get this started. We have a lot of evidence to still gather, and I'd like to get home on time tonight," the other cop says, flipping open a note pad that he pulled from his jacket pocket.

"Mr. Briody." He looks over a file, and then slaps it against the table like it scares me. I'm sure these fuckers have a file of shit I've done over the years. I am no fuckin' angel, and I never claimed to be one. I do what I have to in order to protect my own, and I don't regret a damn thing.

"I see you were arrested four years ago on weapons charges." I nod my head, but don't say a word. These fuckers aren't getting shit from me. I'd rather them lock me up than talk.

"He's already served his time for those charges, Marcus, so why don't you tell us why we are here today?" Mica says with her feisty attitude that I love. She's a wildcat when she goes into lawyer mode, and I love watching her in action.

"Did you kill your ex-wife, Tina Briody?" he asks, watching me.

I roll my eyes at him, and put my hand on the table. He looks at it for a second, and I lean over to whisper in Mica's ear. "I'm about to tell him to go fuck himself." She shakes her head slightly, and turns her attention back to the cops.

"Are you charging my client with murder?" The cop frowns at her, and then looks back at the folder. He reads over a few notes, and then faces Mica.

"Your client admitted that he killed her." Mica turns her head towards me and gives me the death stare. She doesn't say anything at first, but when she turns to look at the cop again, she gives them her wrath.

"Do you have any proof that my client was anywhere near her when the victim was murdered?" They just stare at her without moving. "Is there any hard evidence that he was actually involved in the murder of the victim? Oh, no, you don't?" She looks between them both and then back at me.

"We actually believe that it was his mistress that killed his ex-wife." Her head snaps to me, and then it goes back to them. "You mean the one who ended things with my client months ago? What probable cause do you have that she would try and commit murder?"

"The victim threatened her," one of the cops says quickly. The other closes his eyes, and I can see the anger flash across his features. He didn't want us to know that they knew about Tina threatening my girl.

"And that was in the past. Both parties moved on from that. The child abuse case was dismissed on all accounts. There was no reason anymore to be angry with the victim. Plus, Mr. Briody's mistress had a baby just a few weeks ago. She wouldn't murder someone that soon after giving birth." Mica looks back at me and the cops clear their throats.

"If you're not guilty, then why confess?" Instead of saying anything, I just sit in my chair and stare at them. I don't say a word, and I can see that it pisses them off. I've done this song and dance before, and saying shit either labels you a rat and gets your ass killed, or puts the blame on someone you care about. I won't do either of those things, and I'll do everything in my power to make sure my Trixibella never has to see the inside of a jail cell.

"Well, we are going to hold you and charge you for the murder of Tina Briody." The cop looks at me intently for a few minutes before he leans in and says, "You know you won't see your children while you're behind bars, right? What makes you think that it won't give Miss Rawlins a reason to leave you once and for all?"

"She may hate me ninety percent of the time, but she would never take my kids from me," I state with an even tone. I know he's trying to get me to say something about her, but I won't.

"I hope she's worth a prison sentence," he says snidely.

"Wouldn't you like to know?" I smirk at him. He shakes his head and stands up, pushing his chair behind him.

"Miss. Duncan, I'll leave you with your client. Please let the guard know when you are done so we can take him through the booking process." She nods curtly, and then watches as they leave the room. When the door closes behind them, her head snaps towards me.

"Are you fucking kidding me, E?" She looks ready to murder me, and I put my hand on hers that is on the table.

"Chill, Mica. Your brother was with me last night. He is my alibi, but if I use him, then they are going to lock her up and that shit isn't happening. I want to know who the fuck is framing her and I want the answers now." She stares at me almost in disbelief before she says anything.

"You are an idiot. How do you know that she didn't do it?" I release her hand and stand up from my chair.

"Because Mica, I *fuckin'* know." She huffs out, and looks at me long and hard.

"I don't get what you see in her. You let her ruin your marriage and, even though I didn't like Tina, she didn't deserve your shit." I roll my eyes at her, and take a seat back in the chair.

"Says the girl who tried like hell to get me to end things with her. I finally did, and I'm the fuckin' bad guy. Fuck me," I groan, leaning my head back.

"I tried doing that a long time ago." I snort at her, and she shakes her head. "You're an idiot. I just hope like hell that I'm able to get you off of these charges that you confessed to. She's not good for you, Elec." This time, I stand up and get in her face. Lawyer, friend, or whatever she is to me, I won't let her talk about Trix.

Leaning down so we are eye to eye, I get close to her face. "Don't ever say shit about her. I love her, and there is nothing that is going to stop me from protecting her, even if it's from you. I love you like family, Mica, but you disrespect her again? Don't say I didn't warn you." She shrinks back from me, and I'm glad she does. If she had smarted off like she typically does, I probably would have said some things that I would have regretted.

"E, I love you, but I think you're making a big mistake. I just hope for all of our sakes you know what you're doing. You're going to spend a lot of time in prison. Your kids will be grown before you get out."

I pace the room for a few more minutes before I even say a word. "If doing the time means she's free, then I'll do it." I say, looking across the room at her. She shakes her head and frowns at me.

"You must really fucking love her," she says under her breath. She has no fuckin' clue how true those damn words are. I would take a bullet for Trix if it meant that she would be alive to raise our kids. I haven't done a whole lot of good in the last ten years, but those kids are the best things I've ever done. If taking the rap to keep their mother out of jail is what I have to do, then I'll do it.

"You sign the confession yet?" she asks, writing something on her notepad.

"Yeah." I rub at my eyes and blow out a breath. All is says is that I did it, that I killed my ex-wife to protect my family. No details and nothing more than that.

I watch Mica get up and knock on the door, signaling that we are done speaking. When the cop comes into the room, he cuffs me and leads me back towards the booking area. I wait for fuckin' *ever* to get processed, and then I'm sent to my cell.

Sitting on the shitty ass mattress, I put my head

in my hands and just hope like fuckin' hell that she doesn't go crawling back to that fuckin' prick Romeo while I'm locked up. She may deserve better than me, but I don't give a fuck. I will fight until my last breath to get her and my kids back.

Chapter Eleven

Three Months. Eight Days. Thirteen Hours.

One of the guards comes to my cell to tell me I have a visitor. Getting up from the shitty mattress, I follow him and we make our way towards the visiting area. As they search me and buzz me into the room, I see the families and the men sitting at the tables deep in conversations. I hear little footsteps coming towards me, and I feel his smaller body run into my legs, before I can even prepare for him. "Daddy!" he says excitedly. I pick him up, and I see the guards watching me.

"Hey, buddy," I murmur, squeezing him to my body. Fuck, I've missed him. He looks so much bigger than the last time I seen him.

"Momma and sissy heraw!" He grins at me, and

then points over to where Trix is sitting with a three month old Bexley. Carrying him over to where they are sitting, I set him down on the bench and take my little girl from her mom. Her eyes watch me as I look down at her. A hand comes out like she's trying to grab for me and my heart breaks. If Mica can't get me off, the only way I'm going to be able to watch them grow up is just like this.

"How are you?" Trix asks, breaking the spell that Bexley has over me. I look over at her, and her eyes widen when her gaze zeros in on the black eye that is starting to heal. "What happened?" She stands up and puts her hands to my cheek, checking out my eye.

"Nothing I can't handle, babe," I say quietly. She gives me a look and I shrug it off. I don't need her worried about me. I can take care of myself in here. She doesn't ask anything else about my eye and I'm glad about it. Also, she doesn't know about the shank I took to the side or the hit that was put on me.

"Has your attorney said anything about your case?" she asks. I shake my head no, and continue to look down at my little girl. It isn't the exact truth since I met with Mica yesterday and she told me that she could get me out on bail if the club was willing to put out half a million for my bail. Let's just say I have a feeling that it isn't going to happen because of the shit with Romeo. He'll do everything he can to make sure I say the fuck in here.

"Momma?" Blade asks from his seat. I take the seat next to him and hold Bex close to me. The guard has a soft spot for me, and he doesn't seem to get on my ass when I shouldn't be touching either of my kids.

"Yeah, baby?" She watches me for a second longer before she looks at him.

"Can daddy go home?" She gives him a sad smile, and it fuckin' kills me. I wish like fuckin' hell that I was on the other side of these walls with them again.

"No, baby, he can't. But he'll be home soon, okay?" He frowns at her answer and wraps his arms around one of mine.

Instead of asking her with the words, I give her a look and she frowns. "You can just ask me, you know," she huffs out.

"Fine. Are you back with him?" I grit out. Blade's attention turns to me, and he shakes his head no. Trix looks at him and then back to me.

"No. I'm not. I ended things for good after you got arrested. He was pissed that I chose you over him again. I don't really blame him, though." She looks over at Blade and then runs her hand over Bexley's soft curls. "What I said that day was the truth. You fight for me even when you're not sure you'll win. That's something I want."

Leaning forward, I grab the back of her neck and pull her mouth to mine, kissing her deeply before one of the guards says something. "Briody!" he yells. I pull away from her and grin.

"I love you, Trixibella." She blushes at my words, and it brings me back to when we were still just getting to know each other.

Watching the way she's walking towards me in her

cutoff jeans and skimpy little top, I can see the wicked grin on her face. We still don't do a whole lot of PDA because of my wife who might show up at any minute, but, when she's looking at me like she is right now, I can't help but want to take her right here in the bar area in front of everyone.

"Hey, baby," she purrs, wrapping her arm around my neck, pulling me closer to her sexy as fuck body.

"I was hoping you'd come see me tonight," I murmur against her neck. I run my tongue along her skin, and feel the goosebumps I cause. Her other hand run its way up my back until her fingers are pulling slightly on my hair which pulls my head back. Her lips go to my neck, and she kisses her way down to the top of my shirt. Her other hand slides along my scalp, and she rubs her fingers on the hair that's starting to grow back.

Her lips slide up my neck and to my jaw before they land on my mouth. Picking her ass up, she wraps her legs around my waist, and I walk us towards my room without giving a damn what people say as we pass.

Before I can throw her on my bed, she holds on tightly to me. Her arms are wrapped around my neck, and she's looking at me like I hold the damn world for her. "What?" I ask. She grins at me, and I cup her cheek and pull her lips to mine.

"I don't know why I can't seem to get enough of you," she whispers. Her warm breath kisses my lips, and I lay her down on the bed. She doesn't let me up, so I just run my fingers along her jaw.

"It's because I'm sexy as fuck." I smirk. She shakes her head at me, and I kiss her lips gently.

"You're an idiot." She shakes her head at me again, and I nip at her jaw before moving to her neck.

"I've been called worse." Her moan slips past her lips and her eyes close. I pull away from her enough to get her shirt off of her and, as I'm memorizing her body, I can't help but tell her how fuckin' sexy she is. Fuck, I would give anything to be inside of her right this minute. "So fuckin' perfect," I murmur as I kiss along her chest and stop to the bottom of her bra.

"You're crazy." She giggles, my beard brushing over her skin.

"You're fuckin' beautiful," I say, looking up into her eyes. She blushes and tries to hide her face from me with her hands. Grabbing her wrists, I put her hands above her head, and look her in the eyes. "It's the fuckin' truth. You steal my breath away and you don't even realize it." Her eyes start to

water, and I lean down to kiss her lips.

"I'm falling," she says quietly. All I know is that I'm completely fucked. I never expected to fall for her. Shit, I couldn't even tell my wife that I loved her all these years and the words just almost came out of my mouth. I almost told my Trixibella that I loved her.

"I'll catch you," I whisper before I take her mouth in mine and show her just how fuckin' much I care about her.

Her hand touches my arm, and my mind comes back to the present. "Where were you just now?" she asks. Her eyebrows are scrunched together, and she almost looks worried.

"I was just thinking about the day I almost told you I loved you." An eyebrow rises and she gives me a questioning look. I never told her I loved her until after it was too late, so she has no idea what time I'm actually talking about. "You told me you couldn't get enough of me, and I told you that it was because I am sexy as fuck." She rolls her eyes and me, but I see the small grin that pulls at the corners of her lips.

I waggle my eyebrows at her and I already know what she is going to say. "You mean you're crazy," she says, laughing.

"You said the same thing to me that day." She nods her head, and looks around the room for a few seconds, before she turns her attention back to me.

"I know. I remember it like it was yesterday. I just didn't know that you wanted to tell me you loved me." She looks away almost like it hurts her to say the words.

"I've loved you since day one. I'm an idiot, I know. I let you go when I should have fought harder for you, for them, for us." When Bexley starts to cry, I hand her over to Trix who pulls a bottle out of her bag and mixes some formula into the water and shakes it before handing it to her.

"I wish you were home and not here." She looks around the room again, almost like she's nervous.

"Me too, baby." I reach out to grab her thigh and she looks at me with sad eyes. "Why do you look so nervous?" I finally ask when she doesn't look me in the eye.

"I got a note the other day, and I didn't want to say anything if it was going to affect your case." Blade moves into my lap, and I let him wrap his arms around me.

"Wuv you, daddy," he says, kissing my cheek with a loud smack. I wrap my arms around him and hug him to me. The guard looks like he's about to say something, but the other one stops him.

"I love you too, kid," I say, kissing his cheek. Turning my attention back to Trix, I ask her what the note said.

Leaning forward, she whispers, "That letting you take the fall was the wrong choice." I can feel my anger start to boil over and I curse under my breath.

"Oooh daddy bad wood." Blade says, grabbing my cheeks with his hands. I look back up at Trix and she's looking down at Bex.

"What if something happens while you're here?" Her voice is low and shaky.

"I won't let it. I'll do everything in my power to

protect you three even while I'm locked up," I affirm. She nods her head, but doesn't say anything else. I need to get a call to Prez and make sure he knows that someone is threatening Trix.

Before I can say anything else, the guards are announcing that visiting time is over. Blade hugs onto me, and refuses to let go when Trix tries to tell him that they need to leave. She puts Bexley in her car seat before she pulls Blade off of me.

"I love you, E. Please be careful in here. We need you on the outside." I nod my head and watch Blade as tears stream down his cheeks.

"I love you too, babe. I'll be home soon." Blade wraps his little arms around my legs and hugs me as hard as he can before Trix grabs the car seat, and his hand, leading him out of the room. His tear-streaked face looks over his shoulder at me, and he waves slightly.

My heart constricts and I feel like I'm letting them down. I'm going to rot away in here and they are going to be out there.

When the guard leads me back to my cell, I take

a seat on the extra bed and put my head in my hands. I've already missed the last three months, and I'm going to miss a hell of a lot more. Fuck. Grabbing the phone from under the mattress, I dial Prez's number and wait for him to answer.

"Yeah?" he barks out.

"Someone is threatening her. I want someone to watch them," I demand. I hear his sigh come over the line, and I know he doesn't like when anyone gives him demands.

"I already know about it. She brought it to me when she found it. I got her. I need you out here to figure out who the fuck is trying to frame Trix. Romeo went off the rails when she ended shit with him after you went in, and I am filling in for his ass until he can pull his head out of his. You sure as hell don't deserve me helping with this shit, but she does and so do those kids."

Closing my eyes, I lean back against the concrete wall and breathe in a sigh of relief. That means that Ro won't be sniffing around her for a while.

Chapter Twelve

Three Months. Six Days. Two Hours.

"Briody!" someone yells from outside of my cell. I look towards the doorway, and see one of the guards standing there.

"What?" I bite out. I'm fuckin' bitter that I'm in this fuckin' hellhole, and all I want to do is fuck my girl instead of my damn hand. Hell, I want to see my kids even more than that. I've seen them once a month for the last three months, and it fuckin' burns my chest every time they walk away from me.

My little girl is starting to roll around, and all I have are pictures of the three of them. Blade is now two and a little hellion. He is definitely keeping Trixie busy. Every time I call her, she's practically yelling at him to sit down or to watch the movie that she has on the TV for him.

"You're being released," he states. I stare at him, thinking that maybe he's fuckin' with me.

"What do you mean I'm being released?" I ask hesitantly. I get off my bunk and make my way towards him. If he's fuckin' with me, I'm going to fuckin' kill the bastard right here. I don't give a fuck if I get more time added to my sentence.

"Looks like your lawyer found some evidence that proves that you didn't do it," he says, shrugging. "Let's go. We need to get you processed and out the door." I look back at my cellmate that I was graced with last week and he looks at me with wide eyes. He's a young kid and in prison for attempted murder. He's a good kid that got mixed up in the wrong crowd.

"You know where to find me when you get out. I'm serious. Let me help you get your shit together," I say to him. He doesn't say a word, but he nods. At least I know the fucker was listening to me.

The guards lead me away from my cell and towards freedom. Fuck, I can't wait to get out of this shithole. Six months in lock up feels like a damn lifetime, and I can't wait to kiss my kids and my Trixibella. They are the only things that kept me fighting for my life in this place. A lot of fuckers didn't even think to fuck with me because of my associations to Stavros and the club. His reputation precedes him and, since there has been some chatter about what he went through and what he did to protect his ol' lady, he's even more of a badass to these pussies in here.

The guards process me and hand me my clothes, telling me to strip down and redress in my street clothes. Once I get my shit back, I feel like a new man. Now, I just need a fuckin' shower.

The sun is bright as I make my way through the doors. I look up to the sky and feel the warm rays hit my skin. When I look back down towards the road, I see my angel standing there. Her red hair is blowing, and she's standing there by herself. Her tee shirt and jeans hug her fuckin' body perfectly and I can't help but stand there and stare at her.

Making my way towards her, I feel my heart pounding in my chest. How the hell did she even know I was getting out today? She knew before I did. Wrapping my arm around her, I pull her body into mine and just breathe her in. She wraps her arms around my neck and just holds on to me. One of my hands rests on her lower back and the other is on the back of her neck.

"Fuck, you don't know how fuckin' good it feels to hold you," I whisper against her hair. She nods her head and buries her face into my neck. I can feel her tears as they fall on my skin. "Where are the kids?" I ask, slowly pulling away from her.

"Stavros is watching them," she says with a shy smile.

"So, I get you all to myself?" I ask with a grin. She nods her head and pulls me back to her body. "God, it feels like forever since I've seen you." Since I've been locked up, we've finally been able to just talk. Nothing but talking, and maybe wishing it was her pussy sliding down my shaft as I thought about her at night. My fuckin' hands got a damn work out while I was inside, and fuck if I didn't wish that it was her wrapped around me.

"You saw us a few weeks ago and we talked last night on the phone," she says, grinning up at me. I shrug my shoulders. I could have seen them yesterday, and still I would think that it's been too damn long.

"Am I taking you home?" she asks, running a finger down my chest. I try to remember if my mortgage was paid while I was gone, but I can't think of anything but her.

"Stavros gave me money to keep your mortgage current for when you got out." I pull her mouth to mine and kiss her again.

"Fuck, I don't know what I would do without you." Her hands run through my longer than ever hair, and she pulls at the sides, nails scratching at my scalp. She did this all the time when we would be lying in bed together. It brings back so many memories. We'd fight, we'd fuck, and then we'd make up. It was what we always did. I hate that we fought so much, but she's so passionate that I don't think we could help it. The make-up sex was fuckin' phenomenal, to say the least.

"Oh, I heard a song that reminded me of you the other day," she says, as I lead her towards her car. The same car I paid for when hers broke down on her six months after we started our affair.

"What was that?" I ask, putting my lips against her neck briefly.

"Don't judge," she says with a blush creeping up her neck. I push her up against the car and press my body against hers.

"I would never." I nip at her chin and then her jaw. "Just tell me."

"It's a pop song." She looks over my shoulder, keeping her eyes off of me. I urge her to tell me the name, and I can't help but give her a strange look when she says the name of the song. "*Rock Bottom.*" Her voice is quiet, and I force her to look at me. Before I can ask her why that song remind her of me, she tells me that she wants to play it for me.

I release her and she opens the driver's door and grabs her phone. She searches for something on it by pushing a bunch of buttons on the screen before turning the volume up. I listen to the words and I have to admit that they hit home with us half the time.

When the song comes to an end, she looks up at me expectantly. I pull her back to me, and press a kiss to her lips. “That definitely sounds like us. I just hope like hell that we can figure this shit out for the kid’s sake.”

“Me too,” she whispers, pressing her face into the side of my neck. Her lips touch my skin.

“Come on, let’s get home and away from this fuckin’ place.” I bite down gently on her earlobe and hear her sigh. Grabbing the keys out of her jeans pocket, I walk her to the passenger side and help her in the car. Shutting the door, I take one last look at the prison before I make my way to the driver’s side and get in.

The whole drive to my house is spent quiet, almost like we don’t know how to talk to each other now that I’m out of prison. Her hand is resting on my thigh and, every few seconds, she rubs her fingers in a circle. My hand is in her lap and my fingers are absently rubbing between her thighs.

Out of nowhere, she turns to me and gives me a strange look. She goes to say something, but thinks better of it. Pulling into the driveway, I put the car in park and turn to her. "What?" I ask. She goes to say something, but then closes her mouth again.

"Trixibella, what?" I finally growl. She gets the hint to just fuckin' spit it out.

"Don't be mad, but, with the threats and shit, I didn't feel like me and the kids were safe in my apartment anymore..." She trails off, and I raise an eyebrow at her.

"Okay?" I ask. "So, you moved to another one?" She shakes her head no, and my mind goes straight to my worse fear. She's back with Romeo. "Then what, Trix? I don't feel like playing a fuckin' guessing game. All I want to do is shower and fuck you. So spit it the fuck out," I ground out.

Her eyes narrow at me and she opens her door, getting out in a huff. I get out and follow her as she huffs and puffs her way to my front door. I watch as she unlocks it and makes her way inside. I love when she's pissy like this. This is when we have the best fuckin' sex. The madder she is, the kinkier she gets.

Reaching out before she can go too far into the house, I grab her arm and push her against the wall next to the door. Slamming the door shut, I lean into her and watch her expression. She has three expressions written all over her face: anger, worry, and lust.

"What?" I ask, pressing my hips into her. She looks at the ceiling, and refuses to say anything. Instead of trying to force it out of her, I release her and walk away. Making my way into the living room, I see toys on the floor. Not just the toys Blade left when I got arrested, but a doll and a few girly stuffed animals.

Walking out of the living room, I make my way towards Blade's room. A crib is sitting against the opposite wall as his bed, and there are more toys on the ground. I make my way to the master bedroom, and I see her stuff all over the bed and some of her shoes on the ground by the closet. She moved in here while I was gone. Looking at the dresser by the bed, I see a picture of Blade and me. The next photo is of her and the kids. The last photo is of her and me. It was taken so long ago that I almost forgot about it. It's the only photo we've ever taken, and it's some Polaroid that Harlyn took when she got that stupid camera.

I have Trix sitting on my lap and a beer in my hand. My other hand is between her legs, and cupping her pussy through her jeans. Getting closer to the frame, I pick it up and hold it closer. She has a smirk on her face like she's won something. I hear her footsteps as she makes her way into the room and, when I turn around, she has a small grin on her face.

"You moved in here?" I already know the answer, but I need to hear it from her to believe it. She could have moved anywhere. Hell, I half expected her to leave the damn state while I was away.

"Yeah. I should have told you, but I didn't know what to say or how to even bring it up. I wasn't even sure that you'd be coming home at all." Setting the picture back on the dresser, I make my way towards her. Grabbing the back of her neck, I pull her body to mine and look down into her eyes.

"I fuckin' love you." My breath is on her lips,

and I watch the way her expression changes. She didn't expect those words to come out of my mouth, that much I can tell. She probably expected me to yell at her or something. Start a fight over nothing. Not this time. I'm just fuckin' happy that my girl and my kids are living under my roof.

"That wasn't the response I was expecting," she whispers against my lips. I frown at her response, but I'm sure it's something I should have expected, even though I've been trying to get her ass into my house permanently since before she started dating that prick, Romeo.

"What response did you expect? I've been trying to get you in my house since after the lock down was lifted." I press a kiss to her lips, but she breaks it before it can go too far.

"And what? Live with you and your wife?" She scrunches her nose in a cute way, and shakes her head. "No, thank you. I didn't want her anywhere near Blade. I would have rather been homeless." When she looks at me, her eyes burn all the way into my damn soul. I would have never brought her or my son to live with my wife. Fuck, I would have kicked that bitch out and moved them in.

"You know damn well that I would have taken care of you. I wouldn't have put you anywhere near that bitch." She nods her head and presses her lips against mine. Closing my eyes, I let her take control and set the pace.

Chapter Thirteen

Her mouth is on mine, and my dick is straining against my jeans. It's been way too fuckin' long since I've had her pussy wrapped around me. Pressing her into the wall, I put her hands over her head and claim her mouth. She moves us around until my back is to the wall, and I grin against her lips.

"You taking control?" She nods her head and releases my hands. Her fingers trail down my body towards my jeans where she starts to undo them. Her mouth connects with mine again as we battle for dominance. Her hands get my jeans undone, and pushed down my thighs, in record time. Pulling her mouth off of mine, she sinks down to her knees and takes my dick into her warm, wet mouth.

I love the feeling of her tongue running along the underside of my dick. She bobs her head up and down my shaft. Grabbing the top of her head, I speed up our pace. Fuckin' her mouth is like damn heaven and, if I don't pull out of it soon, I'm going to blow my load way too fuckin' fast. Her teeth graze my dick as she pulls her mouth off of me. Before I can pull her up, she's taking me back to the back of her throat.

"Fuck," I groan out. "I'm going to come if you don't stop now," I grit out. My hand tightens in her hair, and she doesn't let up on me. I watch as she takes me in and out of her mouth like she's on a damn mission. My balls tighten, and I pull her head to me, until I'm at the back of her throat and coming in her mouth. I fuck her mouth slowly as I come down from my orgasm. She looks up at me with a cocky grin as she licks the tip clean.

Grabbing the back of her hair, I pull her up and kiss her hard. Her mouth tastes like me, and I can feel my dick hardening again. Her hands go to my hair, and she tugs on it, as she hops up and wraps her legs around my waist. Walking her over to the bed, I lay her on her back and run my fingers down to her jeans, starting to undo them. Pulling them down her hips and legs, I run my mouth along her skin. She has no damn panties on, and *fuck* it turns me on even more.

She giggles at my expression. Her hands trail down my arms, and stop at the bottom of my t-shirt. I get her pants off the rest of the way, and let them fall to the floor. Her sandals fall with them, and I make my way back up her body to get her shirt off. I'm not taking my time with her. I need to get inside of her right now. I can do that sweet shit later.

She sits up, as I pull her top up and over her head, tossing behind me on the ground. Her hands start to drag my shirt up my body and I help her get it the rest of the way off. Tossing it behind me, I grab her thighs and pull her pussy closer to my dick.

Sliding my dick next her wet pussy, I hear her little moans. Probing at her entrance for a minute, I slam into her with one smooth thrust. Her breath comes out in a whoosh, her fingers digging into my back. Pulling her legs up, and putting my arms under them to hold them in the air, I pound into her with long hard thrusts. Her fingers go to her pussy, and she starts to rub her clit.

Fuck, it's so damn hot when she starts to pleasure herself while I'm fuckin' her. Her head is back, and her eyes are closed, as I watch her make the O face. Her other hand is bunching up the comforter, and her moans fill the room. Just watching her come apart brings me to the edge. It's been far too long since I've had her coming on my dick.

I feel the tightening in my stomach, and I slam into her hard a few more times, before I spill my cum inside of her pussy. Releasing her legs, I let them fall over the edge of the bed, and I collapse on her body, pressing her deeper into the mattress. Her legs wrap around my waist, and her arms go around my neck, when she opens her eyes again. "Fuck, E," she whispers. I move us both up the bed and to the pillows.

Her pussy pulses around me, and I don't ever want to fuckin' leave her again. Fuck. "I've missed you so damn much." I kiss her forehead and then roll over onto my back, taking her with me. Straddling me, she leans down and presses her lips to mine. Kissing her deeper, my hands run up her back and tangle into her hair. Sitting up, I pull her head back, and kiss my way down her neck. Moans slip from her mouth, and I suck on her pulse, leaving a hickey in my wake.

Lying back on the pillows, I get a good whiff of her perfume on the pillowcases. "How long have you guys been here?" I ask. She rests her cheek on my chest, and I wrap my arms around her.

"Since the threats." She sighs, and I feel her finger running over my arm. "Stavros said it would be easier for them to protect the house than my apartment."

"He didn't want to have to shoot up the apartment complex if he didn't have to," she says, leaning up on her elbows. I feel her heartbeat start to race as she thinks about the threats.

"I need to call him," I murmur, brushing a strand of her hair out of her face. She leans into my touch, and I pull her back down to my chest.

"Are you guys going to find out who killed her?" Closing my eyes, I blow out a breath.

"Yeah. I'm going to find the fucker who tried to

get you arrested and made me miss out on six months of my kids' lives. When I find everyone involved, I'm going to kill them." She stills in my arms, but doesn't say anything. She knows that I'm not a good man; she's been through it with me before. She's watched as I put a bullet in the head of a man who tried to fuck with her at the club. She knows what Stavros would do, too. He's a crazy motherfucker, and I'm glad that he's on our side.

"Is this going to be like the whole drug dealer thing?" she asks. She presses a kiss to my chest, and then rests her head back on my skin. I can feel every breath as it fans over my skin, and I'm hyper aware of every move she makes.

"Only if it needs to be, baby." I drag my fingers through her hair and let them rest on her back. "They fucked with the wrong man. They have put your life and our kids' lives in danger. They deserve everything that is coming to them." She blows out a breath, and starts to trace over the tattoos that cover my forearm. I watch her trace over the skull with thorns before she looks up at me.

"I didn't get many more notes after I told you about them. And, when Stavros wanted us to move into the clubhouse for protection, I asked if we could just stay here. We've had someone outside the house at all times and slowly the notes stopped all together." Her fingers stop moving, and I look down at her.

"What?" I ask, brushing the hair behind her ear.

"The back door was open when I came out of the bedroom this morning. I thought that maybe whoever was watching the house today was the one who left it open." Her eyes widen as realization hits her. "Someone was in here," she whispers, her fingers digging into my arms.

Pushing her off of me, I grab my jeans and pull them on. Making my way through every room, I check for any signs that someone was in the house with them. When I come to the living room, I see the note. I only know where to look because, if it were me, I'd put it in the same damn place.

Walking towards the fireplace, I grab the paper that is barely visible from the corner of the painting that my sister brought over here when I moved it.

Opening the paper, I read over the contents and look around the room again.

I'm watching every move you make. If you don't take the fall, I'll kill him and your little brats. I hope you like being alone.

Trix's hand comes around to my stomach, and I feel her body press into mine from behind. Her lips brush against my skin when she asks, "What did you find?" I fold the note back up, and put a hand on hers.

"Someone was in here," I reply, looking around the room again. I notice a small black speck above the picture on the fireplace. "Is there a step stool or something?" I turn to look at her and she frowns. I push her so that she moves and walks away, wearing just my shirt. She goes into the hall closet, and then comes back with a small step stool. Handing it over to me, she watches my every move.

Setting it down by the fireplace, I open it and then make my way to the top of it. Reaching for the camera, I grab it and follow the lines that lead towards the entertainment center. Dropping the camera on the floor, I grab a wood block and smash the fucker.

Someone has been watching Trix and my kids for who the fuck knows how long.

When I look up at her, I can see the fear written all over her face. Pulling the cords out of the back of the Internet router, I toss them on the ground and walk over to her. Grabbing her face in my hands, I look her in the eyes. "I'm here now, babe. I won't let anything happen to you or them. You have my word." A tear slowly makes its way down her cheek and I feel like shit. I've done a shitty job at making sure she was protected, but not anymore. Someone wants to go to war with me, let him or her bring it.

I will destroy anyone who tries to touch one hair on any of my family's heads.

Pressing a kiss to her forehead, I pull her into my arms and hold her for a minute before I make my way towards the room to grab my phone.

Dialing Prez's number, I wait for him to pick up. When he finally does, I can hear Blade's giggles in the background. "Hey, Easy E. You're out."

"Yeah, but I have a situation," I state. I don't bother acting like I don't have other shit to say to him at first. I want to talk about whomever the fuck was watching this place, and how they didn't notice someone sneak in to place a camera in the living room. Shit. What if there are more cameras?

"What is it?" he barks out when he gets my meaning.

"There was a camera in my living room watching my family. How the fuck did someone get past our man on the outside?" I grit out. Trix's hands grip my hips, and she pulls herself closer to me.

"I'll deal with shit on my side. Was that all you found?" he asks. I hear him whisper something to someone else, but I don't hear that person's response.

"A note," I state, getting more pissed every time I think about someone being in this house while they were asleep. Trix's hands on my skin calm me down a little, but there is nothing that will get rid of this anxious feeling.

I've been itching for a fight for the last few months and, right now, I want to fuckin' kill. "What did it say?" he finally asks.

"That he's watching her every move and, if she

doesn't take the fall, he's going to kill me and the kids." I feel her breathing change and her nails dig into my skin. Grabbing one of her hands, I pull her around my body and into my chest. Wrapping one of my arms around her, I hold her tightly to me. Her arms wrap around my waist tightly and she puts her face into my chest.

"Shit. You know who would want her to take the fall for that bitch's murder?" I look down at Trix, but she doesn't look back up at me.

"Ro," I state. Her body tenses and her eyes meet mine. She looks almost panicked. "He wants her. The only way he'll have her is if I'm back on the inside."

"No fuckin' way," Stavros growls. "He wouldn't fuckin' do that to you. He may be pissed that she left his ass, but he wouldn't frame you or her for murder just to get back at you." Stavros will never see what is right in front of him. He's too damn loyal to Romeo and that is a weakness. If I find out he has anything to do with this shit, I don't give a fuck what the rules say, I'll put the barrel of my gun to his forehead and pull the trigger. No questions asked.

"Check the room and see if there are any other cameras. I'll send one of the guys to set up an alarm and some more security. I'll keep the kids here until that shit is taken care of." Fuck that. I want them with me.

"We will just come to the clubhouse. I want to see them." He tells someone to get Dick and to have him come see him before he says anything else to me.

"Fine. Your room is still vacant, so use it for as long as you need." I tell him thanks before I hang up and pocket my phone. Running my hands down her back, I try to soothe her fears the best I can. She knows that I won't let anyone hurt her or the kids, and I'm going to prove it.

Romeo better hope like fuck he has nothing to do with this shit, or I'm going to be gunning for his ass.

Chapter Fourteen

By the time we shower and get dressed, I have a feeling that there are cameras in every room of the house. Walking into the garage, I find the radio frequency detector, and start to scan the whole fuckin' place. I find another one in the living room, two in the kitchen, one in the kid's room, four in the master bedroom and one in each bathroom.

Trix watches as I stomp each camera into the title floor. She looked pale when I found the one in the kid's room. "How long have they been watching?" she asks in disbelief. "Why was there a camera in the kid's room?" She shakes her head, and I see that she's close to breaking down. She's always been strong, so to see this breaks my heart. Not once has she ever crumbled under all the weight that has been on her shoulders.

"I don't know, baby, but I'm going to find out. Most of the cameras were in here, so I think they were watching you." Her body shivers, and then she puts her face in her hands.

"What could I have done to make someone do that? I don't understand." Her voice breaks and when her eyes turn to me, I see all the hurt, sadness and fear. Tossing all the broken cameras into the garbage, I make my way towards her and lean her back on the bed.

"It's not you. It's them. I will find out who's doing this to us, and I will make sure they never come near you or the kids." Her hand reaches out and gently cups my cheek.

"Do you really think that Romeo has something to do with this?" Her fingers run along my new beard, and then make their way up the side of my head. Leaning into her touch, I close my eyes. I don't want her to freak the fuck out.

"Yeah, I do. You left him because of me." She sighs, and then her legs wrap around my hips. "He's wanted you for as long as I can remember and, now that he's had you, he may not stop trying to get you back. Blaming you for the murder of my ex-wife was one way that he knew he could get rid of me. He knows I'd go to jail before I let you go. He knows how much I love you." Her fingers slide through the top of my hair and she blows out a breath.

"Are you going to kill him?" Her question is quiet, and I almost didn't hear her.

"If he has anything to do with this shit, yeah, I won't hesitate." A tear falls down her cheek, and she looks down towards my hips. "I know he means something to you, but if he's the one trying to fuck with you, it's already settled. You know I won't take this shit lightly, especially when it comes to those kids of ours. Stavros can come after me if he wants, but I'll protect what's mine. You are mine. They are mine. Nothing will take you guys away from me."

"Elec," she whispers. Her eyes bore into me, and I can see the understanding in them. She knows I'll do what I have to. "I love you. I'm sorry for making this even more messed up. If I would have stayed away from him like you told me, we wouldn't be in this position." I run my fingers along the side of her face and trail them down her neck.

"If it's not him, then we'd still be in this same position. Don't blame yourself, baby." Leaning forward, I press my lips against hers and claim her mouth. Whoever the fuck put the cameras in here watched her. They watched us fuck earlier, and I'm sure they watched her dress and undress for however long. Hell, they probably watched her while she stuck her fingers into her sweet cunt. Watched her as she fingered that tight pussy, and made herself come, hopefully while thinking about me.

My dick hardens just thinking about her putting her fingers in her sweet cunt, and I kiss along her neck. "Did you pleasure yourself while in my bed?" I rasp out. My eyes watch her as she squirms under me.

"Yes," she says on a moan. I slowly rock my jean-covered dick over her pussy. She's wearing a dress, so it wouldn't take me much to get inside of her right this minute. My dick wants to pull her panties to the side and fuck her rough and fast right now, but my heart wants to go to the clubhouse to see my kids.

"As much as I want to fuck you right this second, I want to see the kids." She grins up at me and wraps her arms around my neck, pulling herself up when I start to stand.

"Good. I miss them already." She gets off the bed and fixes her dress quickly. Adjusting myself, I watch her for a moment. My God, she's fuckin' beautiful. Even after giving birth to two kids, her body is just as fuckin' sexy as it was when I met her. Her tits are a little bigger, and so is her ass, but I ain't complaining.

She grabs my hand and all but drags me out of the house and towards the car.

The ride to the clubhouse is short and, when I pull into a parking space, I see Blade playing on a swing set with Stavros pushing him. "Hey, fucker," he greets. When Blade sees me, he throws himself off the swing and comes running to me. His little legs take him as fast as they can, and I kneel down to catch him when he throws himself at me.

"Daddy!" he screeches in my ear. I hear

footsteps coming towards me, and then I see my little girl. Standing up with him in my arms, I reach out and take her out of Dex's arms. It's fuckin' hilarious to see these two big motherfuckers swinging and holding these two little angels.

"Hey, buddy," I say, pressing a kiss to his cheek before I place one on his sister. "Hi, princess," I coo at her. She grins a slobbery grin and puts her head on my shoulder. Fuck, I missed these two little humans. They are seriously the only things that kept me going in that shit hole, knowing that even if Trixibella and I didn't work out, I would still have these two angels to keep me going.

A hand comes around my waist, and Trix is kissing Bexley's face. She tries to bury her face into my neck while giggling at her mom. "Daddy, Daddy!" Blade says. He grabs my face, and forces me to look at him instead of his sister.

"What?" I ask. He grins at me and wraps his arms around my neck.

"I missed ew!" he says, kissing my cheek.

"I missed you more. I am so happy to be home."

The door to the clubhouse opens, and all eyes turn towards Romeo. He has a scowl on his face and I feel Trix start to pull away from me. I look down at her and frown, but she doesn't take her eyes from him. She doesn't move away from me, but she does take her hands off my waist.

In a way, it might be better to not piss him off too much if it's really him that's leaving the notes. But it still pisses me off to know that he's the reason she released me. His eyes scan over us and then he walks towards his bike without saying a word. We watch as he gets on and starts the engine with a roar. He takes off with a salute to Stavros, and I'm sure he only did that out of respect.

As the rumble of his engine disappears into the distance, I turn back to Trix. Her eyes are still glued to where she last saw him. Leaning towards her, I press a kiss to the side of her head and her eyes shoot to mine. She instantly looks guilty, but I don't say anything.

Her eyes go to Bexley, and she grins a little at her. Looking at Bexley the best I can, I see that she's already asleep. "Come on. Let's put them down for a nap." She runs her fingers though Bex's dark curls and then looks up at me. Nodding my head, I look over at Stavros and he signals for me to leave with her.

By the time we get them both down for their naps, I want nothing more than to find out what the fuck was up with Trix when she watched Ro leave. Grabbing the monitor, I grab her hand and lock the door behind us. Making our way outside, I walk towards the back of the building and stop. My back is to her, and I can feel her eyes on me.

"I know you're mad," she says quietly. This isn't my girl. She doesn't ever get quiet around me when she wants to say something. Typically, she gets in my face just like I get in hers.

"You don't know shit," I ground out. I take a few calming breaths before I even think about turning around. Before I can move, she's moving around me to stand in front of me. Her eyes are facing the ground and I hate it. This isn't her. What the fuck happened?

"I see the look on your face. It's the same look you had when I walked out the door. The look you gave me when I told you I was done." Her hands are clenching at her sides and I just stare at her. She's pissed, but she isn't letting me have it.

"What happened to the woman you used to be?" I ask. I'm honestly curious. The woman I fell in love with was feisty and never backed down from a fight. She went after what she wanted, and she gave everyone hell when she didn't get her way.

"I grew up!" she spits at me. "Someone had to. In case you forgot, someone has to be the parent and raise those two kids inside. We all know that it isn't going to be you." She pokes her finger into my chest, and I narrow my eyes at her.

"You didn't fuckin' grow up. Hell, girl, you've been grown since I met you. You're almost timid and shy now. What the fuck happened?" She flinches away and turns to walk away. "Don't fuckin' walk away," I grit out, grabbing her arm. I spin her to face me and her eyes flash almost in fear.

I soften my voice and wrap my arms around her waist, pulling her body closer to mine. "Baby, please tell me what the fuck is going on."

She sucks in a breath and I ready myself for whatever blow she's about to deliver. "I can't let you kill him." A tear trails down her cheek and before I can ask her why, she continues. "While you were gone, I dropped the kids off with Harlyn for the afternoon while I went to run some errands. I was walking downtown when someone grabbed me from behind. A hand went over my mouth, and I tried to fight him, but I was not strong enough. Before he could pull me into the empty alley, Ro was there. He saved me from getting raped… or worse." More tears are falling down her face now, and I look over her shoulder towards the street.

"He saved me and, if I don't protect him now, I'll regret it." Her lip trembles and the only thing I can do it pull her closer to me. As much as I hate that he was the one to save her, I'm thankful he did. Who the fuck knows what would have happened if he hadn't been there? I feel her shuddered breaths and I can't help but tighten my grip on her.

Losing her forever will be my downfall. I may be a bastard, but she is nothing short of an angel. She's the pure where I'm the evil. *She* saved *me*.

She brought me back from the shitty life I was leading before her. Trix is the first woman to make me feel again even after I shut myself down to the thought of it. I never wanted to find someone else. Shit, I didn't even want Tina. My hand mindlessly runs up and down her back and the only thing I can do is imagine what happened to her that day. A million scenarios run through my head and I keep coming back to the same thing: I could have lost her.

I wasn't here to protect her like I should have been. Instead, I was in prison and I bet that Romeo had something to do with it. He knew he lost her the day the results came in. We all knew it, and I'm sure it fuckin' killed him to know that she was still mine even after everything I've put her through.

Do I deserve her? Fuck, no. Do I want to do right by her? Yeah. I would do anything to make up for that shit in the past up. She deserves the fuckin' world, and

I'm going to be the man to give it to her. I don't give a fuck if that makes me a selfish bastard. I can't live without her. She can be pissed at me, and hate me all she wants, but she will never be anyone else's.

Chapter Fifteen

Two and a half years ago

"I fucking hate you!" Trix yells at me, as she's pulling her dress back on. I ignore her words and get off the bed. When she walks past me again, I grab her around the waist and pull her into my body. "Let me fucking go. You're a goddamn pig." She shakes her head at me, and I just hold her tighter.

"You know, I ain't letting you go. You fight me all you want, but this shit doesn't change. I piss you off and you bitch at me." She huffs at me and I just wait her out.

"You lied. You promised me and look what that got me." She frowns, and I release my grip on her slightly. "You said you were getting divorced. You promised." A tear slides down her cheek, and I use my thumb to wipe it away.

"Slowly, you are breaking me. You have no idea how much it hurts to have the man you're in love with promise you something and for him to change his mind."

I feel my heart constrict at her words, but I don't let me emotions show. She doesn't know how much this shit affects me, too. I had every intention of divorcing Tina.

"It's not that fucki'g simple, Trixie," I growl. She pushes at my chest, causing me to tighten my grip again.

"Yes it is!" she screams at me. She finally gets out of my grip and grabs her bag off the floor. When she gets the door open, I wrap my arm around her waist and haul her back into my body, slamming the door closed.

I spin her around and push her against the wall. "Don't," I warn her. Her face turns into a scowl and she leans forward and bites me. I use my body to push hers into the wall harder and she gives me a dirty look. My hand goes to her throat, but I barely put any pressure on it. I would never hurt her, even if she pissed me off.

Her eyes flash with a look that I haven't seen in a while and it turns me on. Fuck. It's a cross between lust and anger. I love when she puts up a fight. She is feisty, and loves to give it to me just as good as I give it to her.

"She isn't going to let me divorce her. She threatened

to kill herself if I file the papers. I don't want that shit on your conscience. Me, I don't give a fuck if she does it. I know that it will affect you in a different way than it would me. I can deal with that shit, but I don't think you can." She stops struggling against me, and her eyes flash to something I've never seen.

"Is it because you don't think I'm strong enough, or that you're only trying to protect me?" Her eyes are boring into me and I just give her the truth.

"Both." Her eyes soften slightly and she puts her hands on my biceps. Her lips find mine, and I wrap an arm around her waist and crush her body to mine. My hands go under her ass and I lift her up. Her legs wrap around my waist and I move us from the wall. "I will always do everything I can to protect you," I whisper against her lips.

I lay her on the bed and my eyes scan over her face. She doesn't look nearly as pissed as before, but that can all change in the matter of minutes.

"I'll never get all of you, will I?" she finally asks. I have to take a deep breath before I say anything to her.

"You have the important part of me." I grab her hand and put it on my chest. Her eyes follow her hand, and she stares at both of our hands on my heart.

"I wish I had all of you." Her voice breaks and so does my barely beating heart.

"I won't hurt you." I lean down and kiss the side of her jaw. I watch her throat as she swallows, and her next question makes me realize how shitty I've been to her over the last year.

"How do I know you are being truthful? You cheated on your wife with me. How do I know that you aren't going to start sleeping with someone else, too?" I look her in the eyes for a few seconds before I answer her. I want to get a read on her, but I can't. She has a perfect mask hiding her expressions, and I wish I could tell what she was thinking.

"No other bitch comes close to you. I wouldn't have made you that promise if I didn't mean it. You will get all of me one day. You calm me down, you piss me off, and you make me fuckin' crazier than anyone else. I will kill for you."

Her next words are what turn my whole fuckin' life upside down.

"I need to tell you something…" She trails off and I just stare at her. I wait for her to tell me whatever it is. She cups my cheek, almost like she's afraid of losing me.

"I'm… pregnant."

I pull back almost like I've been burned. There is no

fucking way that I could be this kid's father. Fuck. *She's been fuckin' the other brothers still. Shit. Goddammit. I get off the bed and pull my jeans on. I pull on a shirt and my boots, making my way towards the bar. When I get outside of my room, I put my fist through the damn wall. I can hear her squeak through the open doorway, but I don't stop. I just keep moving. I grab a bottle of Jim Beam, and down a few big gulps, before I slam it on the bar. Closing my eyes, I rub my fingers into my eyes and wait for the betrayal to subside. She fuckin' promised that she was done with the rest of the men.*

Fuck this shit. I need to get the fuck out of here.

I spend the next few hours riding around mindlessly. The only thing I can think of is her and that she is pregnant. There is no way that kid can be mine. I made sure I couldn't have kids when I was eighteen. When I finally cool off enough to talk to her, I make my way towards her apartment. When I park my bike, I see her looking through the window at me. I shut off the engine and put my kickstand down. Before I make the trek to her door, I decide that I still want her in my life in whatever way I can get her. If she's just the girl I fuck, then so be it. I'll take what I can get.

The door opens before I even have a chance to knock. She has a scowl on her face, and part of me doesn't care that she's pissed because she's fuckin' one or more of my brothers and the other part of me is fuckin' fuming. I promised her I wouldn't fuck around on her, and I expected her to do the same thing.

I pace the small ass apartment for a few minutes before I even say anything to her. "How far along?" My voice is low and deadly. I can see the fear on her face, and I like knowing that she sees how pissed I am.

"Ten weeks," she replies quietly.

I start to pace again, and my mind races as I think back to ten weeks ago. I've pretty much have had Trix in my bed every night for the last seven months unless I was out of town on a run. Fuck, I start to make my way towards the bedroom to grab my jacket that I left here a few weeks ago. "You're fuckin' shitting me, right?" I ask when I turn to look at her. Judging by the look on her face, I can see that she isn't fuckin' around.

"The baby is yours," she says softly. I don't even think; I just react. There is no fucking way.

"No, it's not. You've still been fuckin' my brothers after you swore to me that you weren't. I told you I wouldn't share you." She comes towards me, and I swear I can see the anger in her face from me not believing her.

She pokes her finger in my chest and gets right in my face. "Fuck you. How dare you accuse me of sleeping with your brothers?" Before she can continue, I stop her.

"You're a fucking club whore. You fuck all the brothers." Before I can even anticipate it, she slaps me. The crack of her hand against my cheek echoes through the tiny ass fuckin' apartment. Grabbing the hand that just hit me, I push her up against the wall. I don't do it hard now that I know she's pregnant. I put her arm above her head, and I lean in really close to her. "Don't ever hit me."

I see the venom in her eyes and it turns me on. "I haven't fucked any of your brothers in the last year and a half." I roll my eyes at her and it pisses her off more. "You are the only selfish son of a bitch that I've slept with in that time frame."

"Then, how the fuck did you get pregnant?" I growl.

"Are you a fucking moron? We have sex almost every fucking night without using protection. I'm surprised I didn't get pregnant sooner."

I narrow my eyes at her, and she pushes against my chest with her one free hand. "There is no way I got your ass pregnant," I tell her again. She gets ready to say something again, but I stop her. "I got a vasectomy when I was eighteen, remember? I told you that shit when we met." Her eyes widen and her mouth drops open as she remembers our conversation. "There is no way that I got you pregnant," I state. She pushes me away from her and I go this time.

"I didn't sleep with your brothers. If you don't believe me, then maybe there is nothing more to say." Her eyes hit the ground and she refuses to look at me. I walk towards her room and grab my jacket before making my way towards the front door. When I look back at her, I can see the tears running down her cheeks.

She doesn't try to stop me, but part of me wishes she would. Although she doesn't like to admit it, she needs me just as much as I need her.

Making my way out of her apartment, I stand a few feet from her door for a couple of minutes. Before I can walk away, I hear her door open. Her footsteps are quiet and almost unnoticeable. Cold hands land on my stomach and trail their way under my tee shirt. Blowing out a breath, I try to calm myself down before I turn around.

"I don't know how to explain this to you, Elec." She presses her face into my back and my hands go to hers on my chest. "But I swear to you that I haven't slept with any of the Draconic Crimson brothers in the last year and a half. When

you said that you wouldn't share, I believed you. I stopped coming around unless you were there."

I don't say anything to that. I just keep looking towards the parking lot. "Please say something, Elec," she whispers.

"What do you want me to say?" I finally push the words out. Right now is the time that I wish I had a bottle of something hard. I need to get drunk. Hell, fuckin' the anger out of me would work, too. Turning around, I force her to walk back towards the apartment. Her eyes flash with slight fear before she masks it.

I don't say a word; I just shut the door behind us. Spinning her around, I push her over the arm of the couch and run my fingers down her back and to the waist of her small ass pajama shorts. Pulling them down quickly, I undo my jeans and pull my dick out. She needs to know that she is mine, and I'm not sharing her with anyone else again.

Grabbing my dick, I slide it up and down her pussy lips a few times before I slam into her from behind. She moans and pushes back into me. My left hand cracks against her ass cheek, and her back arches. "Elec," she whimpers.

I thrust in and out of her at a quick pace, and her hands are gripping the couch cushion tightly. Her moans tell me she loves every moment and it brings me to the edge quickly. I give her ass one more smack before I feel her pussy clamping onto my dick like a vice. Her whole body convulses as she comes around my cock and I thrust into her, riding her orgasm out. Pulling out of her, I lean over her spent body and whisper in her ear, "Am I the only one who has claimed you here?" My fingers run over her puckered hole and she moans slightly, pushing back on my fingers.

When she doesn't answer me, I give her ass another slap. "I want your words," I grit out. My fingers find their way into her pussy, and I gather her wetness and start to massage my finger into her ass. Her breathing deepens and she continues to push back onto my fingers every few seconds.

"Only you," she whispers. I remove my fingers from her and I hear her protest, but I don't listen to her. Gathering up more of her wetness, I work my fingers in and out of her in a scissoring motion until I know she's ready for me.

Once I get her ready for me, I remove my fingers and slide my dick over her hole. Before pushing inside of her, I reach forward and grab her red hair, pulling her upper body back into me. My arm wraps around her chest and her tit rests in my palm. Kissing my way down her neck, I sink into her inch by inch. I feel her fingers dig into my forearm when I pass through her ring of muscle. She finally relaxes completely and I'm able to start to slowly fuck her ass.

It doesn't take me long before I can feel the tightening in my balls. I come quick and hard. My spent body pushes her into the couch and I stand up as soon as I get my bearings back. Pulling out of her, she looks over her shoulder at me and gasps. "Let's go to bed. We can deal with this shit tomorrow." I pick her up, bridal style, and walk her into the bedroom. I set her on her side of the bed, away from the door and she gets under the covers. Walking over to my side, I strip down and shut off the light.

Getting under the covers, I lie on my back and wait for her to cuddle into my body. When she does, I can finally stop my head from racing with all the possibilities of who the father of her kid is.

Chapter Sixteen

I've spent the last two hours with Trix. We've been laying in bed and talking. She wanted to know every fuckin' detail about me being locked up, and the only thing I can think of right now is who the fuck is watching my family. Instead of trying to ignore the questions, I answered every one she has asked. Some of them scared her and others made her laugh.

When her eyes finally close, I slip out of her grip and make my way towards the bar. When I see Stavros standing at the end of the bar, getting a bottle of Johnnie Walker, I make my way towards him. "Hey, Easy E," he says, looking back over the bar. He takes the bottle from the prospect and motions for me to follow him to his office. I go without thinking twice, and I know that he wants to talk about the shit I said regarding Romeo.

Taking a seat in the chair across from his desk, I wait for him to say something. "Your ass is fuckin' lucky that Mica was able to get your confession thrown out. Not that it gave them anything other than the words 'I killed that bitch.'" He grins at me, and I can't help but laugh.

"What? It's not like I knew what happened to her, so I couldn't exactly write a full confession. Plus, I just needed enough proof found to keep Trixie out of jail and you guys were able to do that." He shakes his head at me.

"You are fuckin' lucky the damn judge didn't keep your ass in jail for that stunt," he mutters. I watch him take his bottle and unscrew the cap, taking a long pull from the brand new bottle. "So the cameras… you get anything on them? A model or serial number?" I shake my head no and he passes me the bottle. Taking a long swig, I set the bottle back on his desk and wait for the warm liquid to hit me.

The permanent scowl on his face tells me that Harlyn still isn't talking to him. He's been watching her from afar since she left and I feel bad for the fucker. He loves her and being away from her still, after everything they both went through, is tearing him apart from the inside out.

"Who would want to get rid of you?" he asks. I give him a look and he frowns. "Besides my VP." Fuck, if I knew the answer to that, I wouldn't be fuckin' sitting here in his office. I would be finding the son of a bitch, and putting a bullet through the fucker's skull.

"You piss any bitches off enough to frame your ol' lady and kill your ex-wife?"

"Fuck, no. The bitches I've fucked over the last few months never got more than my dick for an hour or so at the most. None even knew I had kids or Trix. The only one that makes sense is-" He cuts me off before I can even say his name.

"There is no fuckin' way he would set you both up for that shit." He grits his teeth, and I can tell I'm pissing him off.

"Then bring that cocksucker back in here and

have him tell me to my face that he has nothing to do with this shit. He is the only one that doesn't want Trixie and me together. He's the one that's pissed that Bex is mine and not his." Prez leans back in his chair, and I can see the wheels spinning in his head. He doesn't want to listen to me about Ro and I get that because they are like brothers. But he can't just ignore me either.

"Fine, I'll talk to him. If I don't find reason to believe that it was him, then you need to back the fuck off." He stares at me and I give in, nodding my head. Trix made me promise not to kill that fucker if it *was* him and I'm going to grant her that, for now. If shit proves that he's the one that made me lose time with my kids, then there is nothing that will stop me from going after him.

My phone starts to ring and, when I pull it out of my pocket, I see Trix's number on the screen. "Yeah, babe?" I answer on the third ring.

"Are you coming back soon?" Her voice is quiet and it makes me nervous.

"Why?" I ask, looking up at Prez.

"I just need you," she whispers. Her voice cracks, and the hairs on the back of my neck stand. I get out of the chair without another thought and make my way towards my room. Prez is right on my heels as I come up to my door and swing the fucker open. When we get into the room, I see Trix's hands duct taped behind her back and a note taped to her thigh. I scan the room, see Blade still sleeping soundly, and Bexley is in her crib watching us.

Prez checks the bathroom, and I make my way over to Trix. Pulling my knife out, I cut the tape and slowly pull it from her skin. She whines a little when I rip a piece off of her. Ending the call on her phone, I pull her body to mine and just breathe her in. "Who the fuck did this to you, Trix?" Stavros growls.

He picks up Bexley and brings her over to Trix as she takes a seat on the bed. I grab the note from her thigh and open it.

I am closer to you than you know. I can get to them no matter where you hide them. I will get what I want if it's the last thing I do.

She doesn't answer him, and I can see the tick in

his jaw as he waits for an answer. "Who did this baby?" I ask, as calmly as I can.

"I have no idea. I was asleep when he came in here. He had a mask on." I look over at Prez and he frowns.

"You didn't see any tattoos or anything that would make you recognize him? A smell? Fuck... anything?" he grits out. I cut him a look, and he doesn't say anything. I kneel in front of her and force her to look me in the eyes. I can see the scared look in her eyes, the same one she had when we talked about almost being attacked.

"Babe, did you notice anything? Did you fight back and scratch him?" Her eyes light up and she nods her head.

"I scratched him when he was trying to tie my hands behind my back." She points down to her forearm and Bex starts to cry. I take her from Trix, and she tucks her face into my neck. I run my hand up and down her back until she falls back to sleep.

"I'll get all the men here and check them for any scratches. We might have to put you guys in hiding till we figure this shit out." Trix scoffs at that, and I silence her with a look.

"Fine. Let me know what you find out," I bite out. I watch him walk out the door, turn my attention back to Trix, and I see the frown on her face.

"That note says that nothing is going to keep this guy from us. Why put us in hiding if it isn't going to do anything?"

"It might be safer to keep you guys out of sight. We don't fuckin' know who got in here. We will find the fucker." Her hands grab my face, and force me to look over at her.

"I don't want them touched by this. I know the type of men you and Stavros are. I've seen the damage you've done before, and I've heard about what happened when Harlyn and Stavros where with…" she trails off. My mind flashed back to the damage she is talking about. When Trix and I started fuckin', she worked at a strip club as a dancer in addition to coming to the clubhouse to fuck the brothers and me.

Ever since the day I met her, I've had this crazy protective streak for her and I hated knowing that she was fuckin' anyone other than me. I ended up putting a stop to it when I couldn't take that shit anymore. I had her quit the club, and I was the only one allowed to take her to bed anymore. I refused to share her anymore.

The damage she's talking about was right before I forced her to quit the club.

Walking into Letti's Gentleman's Club, I see my girl on the stage. Her shift started twenty minutes ago, and I would have shown up before she got up on stage, but I got stuck with a fuckin' run that one of the brothers flaked on. The fucker said his ol' lady was having a baby, and couldn't leave her side. Pussy whipped bitch.

Trixie is sliding down the pole as I walk towards the stage to take my seat. When her eyes see me, she gets a relieved look on her face. Her eyes move towards some fuckin' prick sitting at the other end of the stage, and I already know that there is going to be trouble. Grabbing my phone out of my pocket, I dial Tarek's number and tell him to stop by before I kill some fucker at the club.

His response is quick and I know that he's going to be here before I can do anything. If anyone has ever had my back, it's been him. We've been thick as thieves for as long as I can remember. Hell, we've been through a lot of shit in our pasts and there is no one I would rather have on my side.

She crawls towards me, and I pull a hundred from the stack of bills I pulled out of my pocket and lean closer to her. The loud music is blasting in the speakers and the only fuckin' thing I can focus on is her. Her sexy as fuck red hair is curled and spilling down her back in long, loose waves. The tiny black garter set against her pale skins gives me a hard on. I love when she wears black. Her barely there g-string leaves little to the imagination. My eyes scan her body, and I notice the bruise on her thigh.

I go to stand up, but she puts a hand on my chest and pushes me back into my chair. "Not here," she whispers. I tuck the bill in her garter, and her hand comes to the back on my head. Her fingers run along the shaved side of my head before she grabs ahold of the longer top and pulls my head back.

"You better tell me who left this mark on you." She

nods slightly, and puts her tits in my face.

By the time Tarek finally shows up, Trix is done on stage and I was watching the fucker at the other side of the stage who was staring at her. He looked pissed when he saw the way she was with me. If I was a betting man, he's the fucker who put his hand on her.

"What the fuck was so important?" he bites out. He must have been getting laid to be this big of a dick.

"She has a bruise on her thigh that wasn't there this morning. So, unless you want to let me kill the motherfucker, I suggest you stick around a little while." He shakes his head and leans back in his seat. He knows my temper, and me, especially when someone touches what's mine.

"Fuck, I don't get why you don't just claim the bitch already. You fuckin' act like she's your property." I look at him, and I can see the grin starting to form on his face. Dick.

"I am," I grunt out. Some bitch comes around with drinks and sets two in front of us. She winks and I just ignore her.

"You can't claim her if you already have a wife, dumb fuck," he barks out in laughter.

"I can do whatever the fuck I want," I growl. Before he can say something else fuckin' stupid, she comes strutting

out of the back in a bustier and these boy shorts that cling to every curve of her ass. As she's making her way towards me, the guy from the other side of the stage intercepts her. She pulls back from him, and he tightens his grip on her. Getting up, I make my way towards her. Her eyes meet mine over his shoulder. I grab his shoulder, and he turns around to look at me.

"What the fuck do you want?" he spits. His accent is heavy, almost like he's Russian or something. Trix tries to get out of his grip, but he doesn't let her go.

"I want you to get your hands off my girl." He looks me over, and then turns to walk her somewhere else. I grab his shoulder again and, this time, I don't say a word. When he turns, I punch him. He lets her go and I grab her arm, pulling her behind me. His eyes land on me and he comes at me. Pulling my knife out of my pocket, I put it into his thigh. He yells out something in his native tongue, but I have no fuckin' clue what it means.

His hands go to his thigh and he starts to talk shit. Before he can say too much, I raise my knife up and point it at him again. "You go near her again, and I won't hesitate to put this in your throat." The bouncers grab him and pull him out of the club. I can still hear him yelling as they pull him away, but I don't give a fuck. I now have her in my arms, so nothing else matters.

By the time we leave for the night, I know that fucker is going to come at me. I can feel it in my gut when we walk outside the club. When I lead Trix over to my bike, I can hear his footsteps behind me. I see Tarek come closer, and I turn before he can strike. Trix yelps in the background, and I grab the asshole's arm and snap it over my knee. The bone cracks and he screams out in pain. I push him away from me, and I feel her hands on my back.

"Oh my god," she breathes.

He gets up again with the knife in his other hand. He comes at me, and this time I take the knife from him easily and I jam the fucker in his neck. Blood squirts onto Trix and me. She starts to scream, but Tarek puts his hand over her mouth to quiet her down. I don't need anyone else seeing this dickhead on the ground. I grab his arms and drag him towards the back of the building and pull out my phone.

"Yeah?" Prez barks out.

"I need clean up." I don't give him any more than that and my location.

Chapter Seventeen

My phone beeps and when I look down at the screen I cringe. "Hey Mica," I answer.

"Hey, asshole. I'm pulling up to the clubhouse. I need to talk to you." I wrap my arm around Trix in a protective manner, and I don't even know why. She looks up at me and gives me a questioning look, but I ignore it.

"Alright, I'm here." She hangs up without another word, and I go over to wake up Blade. I don't want them left alone again. Trix grabs Bexley and comes back over to me. We walk with both of the kids towards the bar area, and I see Mica already standing there talking to Prez and Romeo. Trix's hand touches my waist and she looks up at me with a questioning look.

Walking straight towards them, I come to a stop in front of Mica and Romeo. "Hey asshole," she greets me. She looks over at Trix and sticks her hand out. "You must be the woman who this fucker would go to jail to protect." She doesn't say it nearly as badly as I expected her to. I expected more venom in her voice than there is right now.

"I have a name," Trix says, grabbing my arm. Mica grins and looks back over at me.

"I know you do. Trixibella Marie Rawlins, thirty year old *single* mother of two beautiful children. You worked for Letti's Gentleman's Club a few years before you gave birth to your first child: Elec Blade Briody Jr. He looks an awful lot like his daddy. And this little one…" She pauses and brushes her fingers gently over Bexley's face.

"This little beauty is Bexley Makena Briody." I notice the way Ro flinches at the mention of Bexley's last name. He still wants her to be his. This adds to the fact that he might be in on it.

"Congratulations, you can read a file." Trix deadpans. I can't help but chuckle at her response. "Does that make you some kind of genius? Or just good at reading?" I can see the smirk on Mica's face and I just wait. Trix doesn't need me to fight her battles for her, and she wouldn't want me to.

"I like you," she finally says after watching Trixie. "This asshole needs someone who will put him in his place every once in a while." She comes closer to me, leaning in to whisper in my ear, and I feel Trix tense besides me. "I take back what I said when I first saw you in jail." She pulls away and, when I look down at Trix, I can see the jealously written all over her face.

"Told you, you were wrong," I murmur. She smacks me in the arm and Blade wants me to let him go. I set him on his feet and he runs over to Prez. Prez picks him up, and wraps his arms around him. Trix pushes her way in between Mica and I. I wrap my arms around her and Bex, pulling them both closer to my body. Ro looks away from us, and then says something to Prez, before walking away.

Bexley reaches out and grabs a piece of Mica's

hair and tugs on it roughly. I grin and Mica doesn't even let it faze her. She's always been great with kids.

"So, what are you doing here, Mica?" I finally ask. Prez hasn't said a word, and it makes me nervous.

"They found some evidence and I need to go over it with you." I nod my head and release Trix. Before I follow behind Mica towards the back room, I kiss Trix on the lips.

"I'll be right back." She goes to say something, but I kiss her again to silence her. "Don't question it. She means nothing to me. You are the only woman who matters to me." Her eyes never leave mine and, when she finally nods at me, I leave her standing there with Prez and the kids.

Walking into the spare room that is used more as a place to fuck than anywhere else, I see the look on Mica's face. She looks uncertain of the information that she's about to share and it makes me nervous. "What is it, Mica? You typically don't have this gloomy look on your face when you want to talk about my cases."

She blows out a breath before she puts a file in front of me. "I know you probably don't want to believe this, but the pictures don't lie." I reach forward and grab the file off the small table that she's standing next to. Opening it, I see a stack of photos. I scan through them quickly, and I have to keep myself from blowing up. She fuckin' lied to me.

Grabbing the most incriminating one, I storm out of the room and grab her by the arm, forcing her into my room with me. Once I slam the door behind us, I push her against the door. "What the hell is your fucking problem?" There's the girl I've been missing. She's pissed that I all but dragged her ass in her. Good thing Dex was holding Bex when I went out there.

"You fuckin' lied."

She scoffs at my statement and glares at me. "What did I lie about?" She's seething mad now and is pushing me away from her. I hold up the picture and her eyes meet mine. "That bitch brought you photos to try and pit you against me and you fucking fell for it. Un-fucking-believable." She shakes her head and then looks back at me. "I fucking hate you."

"You hate me?" I grit out. She just stares at me, not even scared of my anger. She's seen it plenty of times, but right now she doesn't know how close I am to actually doing something about it. "I'm not the fuckin' one who's been fuckin' lying. You want me to look like a damn fool to all of my brothers and friends, fine. Do it. I hope you go down for this shit."

"Are you fucking serious?" she yells at me. "You think I tied my own hands behind my back? That I would put my own kid's lives in danger just to prove a damn point to your arrogant ass?"

"I know you'll do what it takes to protect them, even if that means taking them away from me." My voice is low and deadly. She flinches almost like I actually hit her. Her expression hardens, and she punches me in the junk.

I suck in a breath and fall into her body. I swear I'm going to spank her ass so fuckin' hard when my balls don't feel like they are going to explode. The throbbing pain has me saying fuck at least a dozen times. After a few deep breaths, I try to stand up, but the pain is still radiating in my nut sack. When I finally stand to my full height, I grab her by the neck and push her into the door. "You're fuckin' lucky I love you." She gives me a dirty look, but doesn't say anything.

"What the fuck is your problem?" She continues to stare at me like I'm the one who hit her in the fuckin' cunt.

"You. You are my Goddamn problem. You deserved that for thinking that I would do that and take your kids from you. Are you that much of a bastard? How could you even say those words to me? I've done nothing to make you think that I would do such a thing even if you deserved it. I love you, Elec, and if that meant going to jail to protect you, I fucking would. If it meant that I would protect them? I would gladly do it. The photo is old. Look at the tattoo missing on my thigh if you don't believe me. You were there when I got it done." My eyes scan over her face, trying to figure out what I believe and what I don't any more.

Her pulse quickens under my hand, but I don't pull away from her yet. I'm still fuckin' pissed that she would even punch me in the dick. My other hand slides up her leg, catching the bottom on her dress, pulling it up so I can see her thigh. The memory of her getting inked pops into my head.

Trix wanted to get a tattoo that meant something, so here we are at my buddy's tattoo shop. Calum is a fuckin' wicked good tattoo artist, and the only one I let work on me anymore. Walking straight to the back, I see him leaning over a drawing table. He's been working on the piece for Trix for the last week or so, and I can't wait to see what he came up with.

When he sees me, he grins and holds up the picture. I hear her suck in a breath and, when we get closer, she reaches out to touch it. The roses match the ones on my arm, and I can see the small parts of her that she wanted incorporated into it.

"What do you guys think?" His slight Yorkshire accent isn't nearly as noticeable as when I first met him, but it makes Trix smile.

"I love it. It's perfect," she whispers, still in awe of the drawing. He motions to the chair and she takes a seat. She looks nervous, so I sit next to her and grab her hand.

"You know you don't have to get this done," I

whisper against her hair.

"I want to. It was my idea." She gives me a beaming smile and I relax a little. I don't like seeing her in pain, so the next few hours are going to be like fuckin' torture.

When I look back at the photo, I don't see the tattoo on her skin. This photo is either a fake, or it's from before we were together. She got the tattoo not long after we started to fuck on the regular. I slightly release my grip on her neck and her hands cup my face.

"If this is ever going to work, we need to start trusting each other. You can't assume that lawyer is going to know the truth. She only knows the facts in front of her. The photo tells the truth and we both know it. Calum knows when he put that on my skin. It was before I found out I was pregnant." Her eyes soften, and I can't help but crush my lips to hers. Her arms wrap around my waist, and I release her neck, pulling her body to mine.

My balls still ache, and there is no way I'll be getting it up after that shit she pulled.

"I'm sorry," I whisper against her lips when I break our kiss.

"I think I need to write this date and time down to remember it. You've never once said sorry to me." She has a small grin on her face, and her arms tighten around my neck.

"You'll probably never get it again, either." I bite her bottom lip and suck it into my mouth. "Let's go show her the proof that you weren't involved with those photos recently." She nods and kisses me once more before she releases me.

Walking out of the room, I feel everyone's eyes on us. Some of the guys have smirks on their faces because they probably think I just got done fuckin' her and the ones who saw me drag her ass out of the room know that whatever was the problem is now done. My arm is wrapped around her neck, and she doesn't even look embarrassed. If anything, she looks ready to take on anyone.

When we reach Mica, I can see the confusion

written all over her face. She thought that the photo was going to get me away from Trix. "What's going on?" she asks finally. I motion back to the room and, once she starts to walk over there, I motion for Prez to follow. He sets Blade on the ground, and Trix walks him over to lie him down on the couch. The kids are both tired, but I don't trust them in my room alone until we figure out who tied her up.

The door shuts behind Prez, and Mica turns to face us both. She looks shocked when she notices him in the room, too. "Why those pictures?" I ask. Her eyes dart between us before she slips her lawyer mask on. Her cool, calm and collected mask does nothing for me this time.

"They were given to me. They prove that she's lying to you, E." I walk closer to her and I see the shift in her body. My eyes scan over her like they've done a million times before. She swallows and reaches out slightly to touch me. Moving away from her, I see her eyes change.

"She isn't lying to me. You made me think she was just to drive us apart." She shakes her head no, and looks over my shoulder at Prez. "What you don't know is that she has a tattoo on her thigh, the thigh that is shown in the photo. She's had it most of the time we've been together. I watched her get it. It matches the one of on my arm." Mica's eyes scan over the tattoos on my arm. She knows how much they mean to me. I can see her mind working as she figures out why Trix has them on her, too.

"No," she whispers. Her eyes shoot up to mine and I just watch her. I don't say anything more, and she doesn't move from the spot she's rooted to.

"Why the photos?" Stavros barks out. He looks pissed, and I'm just glad I'm not on his bad side today.

"I wanted her out of the picture," Mica says, quietly. She looks over at me again, and I can see the hurt written all over her face. "I've loved you for so damn long, and you've never given me the time of day." Her eyes focus on the floor and her next words kill me. "I've been invisible to you since the day you met her. She took you from me. I knew Tina never had you. Getting rid of that whore was the easy part. She never held your heart. But I saw the way you changed when you met that whore." She shakes her head, and then raises her eyes to me.

"She's not good enough for you. I tried to make you see over the years that she was nothing. The problems you had together were attempts to get you away from her poisonous ways. She makes you something you don't even recognize. You're not you. You're someone even I don't recognize."

I see the hate in her eyes now. This isn't the girl I've known most of my life. She isn't the same girl who is my best friend's little sister. Grabbing my phone out of my pocket, I send a text to Tarak. Him and me need to talk. We need to talk about what's going to happen to her.

"I'll keep an eye on her until you can talk to her brother," Stavros says from behind me. I nod my head without looking back at him.

"He'll hate you if anything happens to me." Her voice is broken and defeated. She knows how tight Tarak and I am, but she's right. He won't forgive me if something happens to her.

Instead of answering her, I make my way out the

door. I don't bother looking back at her. I know the look she'll give me. She'll beg me for forgiveness and I'll end up giving in.

When I walk out of the room, my phone starts to ring. Looking down at the screen, I see his name, and I take a deep breath before I put it to my ear.

Chapter Eighteen

"Hey, Tar," I say reluctantly.

"What's up man?" He almost sounds like he's bracing himself for something.

"We need to talk. Can you stop by the clubhouse? I'd rather do it in person." I hear him blow out a breath on the other end of the line.

"It's my sister, isn't it?" he asks. His voice breaks, and I can hear shuffling in the background.

"Yeah. She's got some shit to explain," I answer. I know it's not enough to give him an idea of what's going on, but it also doesn't keep him from not showing up.

"Is she…" He trails off like he doesn't even want

to know the answer himself.

"Don't know. Just head down here, and we can talk about the shit I know about. Then, we can talk to her together." He agrees quietly before he hangs up the phone. Pocketing my phone, I make my way over to where Trix is sitting with both kids. The guys are standing around the bar, waiting to hear the word.

"Is she the one who killed her?" Trix asks on a hushed whisper. I wrap my arm around her, and she rests her head on my shoulder. Blade's head is lying on Trix's thigh, and Bexley crawls into my lap.

"I don't know. I need to talk to her, but I need to talk with Tarak first." She nods her head against my arm. I love that Trix doesn't ask me anything other than that. She trusts me to take care of everything, and I will. I'll never let anything happen to them.

"Do you think that Stavros and Harlyn will ever figure their shit out?" Her question doesn't surprise me. It's something I've wondered for a long time, but we don't talk about her since she's been gone. I witnessed the changes in Stavros when she came back, and the even more drastic changes when we found him. He isn't the same man he was before, not that I blame him. I saw the difference in Trix when Dex brought her back from being held hostage. She changed in just a few short hours with that fucker and his lunatics.

"I don't know, babe. I sure hope so." She sighs, and I put my hand on her thigh. "But I get why he's out for blood since she's left. I did the same thing when I lost you. I took it out on every fucker here, but then you were in his arms, and it was too fuckin' hard to stand back and watch you two together."

She looks up at me and her eyes burn into me. "That's why you went nomad." I nod, but don't say anything else. There is nothing else to say. It's true. I ran because I couldn't face the fact that she might not be it for me. Well, I take that back. She is it for me, but I may not be it for her. "It broke my heart that you left without a word. Why didn't you tell me?"

I kiss the top of her head and look towards the front doors. "Because saying goodbye to you has never been an option for me."

She turns to me and gives me a watery grin.

"That is the sweetest thing I've ever heard come out of your mouth." Leaning over, she presses her mouth to mine and kisses me. My hand grabs the back of her head and I hold her mouth to mine.

"Don't get used to it." She smiles against my lips and I can't help but grin, too.

"I wouldn't dream of it. I love the asshole you are." I slip my tongue into her mouth, and kiss her without a care in the world. The only thing I care about right now is her and the kids. They are my end game. No matter what shit I'm dealt with in the future, I'll be okay with them by my side.

Thirty minutes later, the front doors open and I watch Tarak walk in. I feel Trix's body tense up as her eyes watch him. She's spent a lot of time with Tarak and me over the years that we've been together and, although they aren't the best of friends, they have always been friendly. When I go to stand up, her hand doesn't release mine. I look down at her, and she has a strange expression on her face. "What's going to happen?" she asks quietly.

"Don't worry about it. I'll deal with everything,"

I whisper in her ear before kissing the side of her neck. Bexley's legs fall onto the couch cushion next to Trix. Walking over to Tarak, I take in his expression. He knows that shit for his sister is bad if I'm calling him in here. We don't let shit like this go. She is a traitor in our eyes, and there is nothing that can save her now. But, being Tarak's best friend, I'm going to let him know the truth before shit goes down.

"Follow me," I say before I turn on my heel and walk towards the game room. All the men are still by the bar, just waiting for someone to pass along the verdict. They are antsy to do something. Sure, we don't take pride in hurting women, but sometimes you have to do what you have to in order to protect what's yours.

When he walks through the door, I shut it behind me and turn to face him. "What did she do?" he asks. His hands are fisted at his sides, and I know that he's not going to take the news sitting down. He's more likely to swing on me than anyone else I know. We've been through a lot over the years, and there is nothing I want more than to make this shit go away, but I can't. I have to think about my club and my family.

"She killed Tina." He blows out the breath that he was holding and looks up at me.

"What else? You wouldn't have called if that were it. You're glad that bitch is gone. I know that for a fact." I nod my head, because he is right. I am glad that bitch is dead. I would have killed her myself if she didn't leave my family alone.

"She admitted to trying to get rid of my ol' lady. She wanted her out of the picture, so she could have me. She's been scheming against Trix for who the fuck knows how long. She was pissed when I took the fall for the murder, and she did everything she could to try and prove that Trix did it. Hell, I almost believed her bullshit." He shakes his head, and looks towards his hands that are still clenching at his sides.

"You're going to let them kill her over that?" I shake my head no and I wait for him to say something else. "She's like your damn family, E!"

"She was. Not anymore. She helped someone get into the clubhouse. I found my ol' lady tied up in my room. I'm doing what I have to in order to protect what's mine. My girl put up a fight, so as soon as I find out who her partner is, I'm going to kill the motherfucker, too. They could have taken my kids, and there is nothing that is going to make me forget that shit. She knows exactly how I feel about Trix and the kids so, for her to do this, it's deliberate."

He shakes his head at me and grabs something out of his pocket. Before I can react, he swings on me. I take a right hook into the side of my face and fall to the ground. Getting up, I see that he has something in his hand that he hit me with. Fighting dirty is something I've never done. He comes at me again, and this time I hit him in the gut with a knee before I throw a punch into the side of his head.

He falls to the ground and when I walk over to him, I can feel the side of my side starting to swell. "You're my family, too, Tarak. Don't throw that shit away because your sister is a traitor. She made her bed, and she knew exactly what the consequences were before she did that shit. You do, too." He sits up on his arms and looks up at me from the ground.

"Can I talk to her?" I nod my head and reach a

hand down to help him up. If it were my sister on the chopping block, I would do the same damn shit that he did. I don't blame him; he is protecting the only family he's got left.

I lead him towards the room that Prez is still in with her and open the door. I watch as he walks inside and he eyes Stavros. Even Tarak knows he's no match for Stavros. No one around here is, especially when they hear about the shit he went through to save Harlyn's life.

He walks past Stavros and I shut the door, closing us into the room together. I stand beside Stavros and watch Tarak walk closer to his sister. When her eyes meet me, I can see the anger and hurt in them. She knew what she was doing when she tried to frame Trix, and helped someone get into the clubhouse to tie her up, so there is no saving her now. I sure as hell won't.

"What the fuck did you do?" Tarak yells at her. She flinches back from him, and then her eyes meet mine again. She scans my face and frowns when she comes to my jaw. I'm sure a bruise is already forming, but I'll live.

"He's lying." *Of course* those are the first words out of that bitch's mouth. I grab the picture out of my back pocket and walk over to her and Tarak. I hold the photo up and her eyes widen. She didn't think that I would keep the photo in question?

"Mica, you were trying to tell me that Trix was stepping out on me. You showed me this picture from before her and I were together just to get me pissed off enough that I would leave her. You don't think she's good enough for me, so you killed my ex-wife just so you could frame Trix." I take a step back and Tarak's eyes land on me. He doesn't say anything, but I can read him like a damn book. He's pissed that I'm calling her out on her bullshit.

"Who did you help get in the clubhouse to tie her up?" I growl. She turns her head away from me, and looks over at the wall, ignoring my question. I wait a second before I ask her again. "Who the fuck helped you, Mica?" I demand. She flinches at my tone, and I see the look on her face. She isn't scared of me, not at all. When she looks at Tarak, I can see the disappointment written on his face.

Walking over to her, I put the photo in my back pocket and grab her face. Tarak comes towards me, but Stavros stops him. "Don't get in between this unless you want the same fate as your sister." Stavros's threat gets Mica to look at me.

"Give me a name. So help me God, if someone hurts any of them, you'll wish you never met me." My face is an inch from hers. I can see the sweat starting to bead on her skin and feel the way she's starting to shake. My fingers are gripping her jaw hard enough to leave bruises, but I don't give a fuck at the moment. The only thing I want to know is who I'm going to kill for touching what's mine.

A slight knock on the door brings my head away from Mica's. When I turn to look at the door, I see Trix standing there, looking unsure. Her eyes widen when they take me in. A hand comes into the side of my face, and I grab the bitch by the throat causing her hands to grip my forearms instead. "Please," she begs as I cut off her air supply. She starts to gasp, and I feel a hand on my back. When I turn to look at Trix, I can still see the uncertainty on her face.

"I need you to go," I say through gritted teeth. I won't let her see this.

"No." Trix's voice is strong and lets me know she won't back down.

"I won't let you see this. Go!" I demand. She shakes her head at me, and then puts her hand on my arm that's holding Mica by the throat.

"I need to ask her something." I stare at Trix for a moment before I release my grip on Mica's throat. Mica gasps for air, and she falls to the ground at my feet. Trix's eyes never leave mine and she is seriously testing my patience right now.

"Hurry the fuck up. I need answers and she sure as hell won't tell you want you want to know." Trix pushes me out of the way and I wrap an arm around her. I won't let her get too close to Mica. She thinks she can talk to her, but there is no way that Mica will say anything to her. Mica hates Trix more than I ever imagined.

"Are you the one who had that man attack me?" Her voice wavers a bit with her question. I know she's still shook up about that, and I've been too preoccupied to talk to her about it. *Fuck.*

"You're fucking lucky that Romeo was still hung up on you, following you around like a lost puppy dog when you left him for E. He's just as pussy whipped over your whore ass as E is. It's fucking pathetic," Mica sneers at Trix. Trix starts to move forward, but I hold her back against my body.

"You sent someone after my ol' lady while I was in jail?" My mind is racing with a million fuckin' questions. Why the fuck would she do that? "Because I took the fall, you sent someone after her?" I can feel my heart rate increase, and my hands are itching to get back around her neck.

"She doesn't deserve you, E! Why the fuck can't you see that? You and I were always together. It was supposed to be me and you, just like when we were growing up." She launches herself at us, but Tarak grabs her, pulling her back and pushes her into the wall.

"You seriously sent someone to hurt her?" Tarak gets in her face, and I have a feeling that he won't go easy on her. He once dated a girl who was sexually assaulted. It happened while they were together and, ever since then, he's closed himself off from relationships afterwards. "What the fuck was your plan, Mica? For that fucker to kill her or just rape her?"

I feel Trix flinch in my arms, and I hold her tighter to my body. My lips go closer to her ear and before I can say anything, she turns to look at me over her shoulder. Our faces are an inch apart. "What if he was successful? Or, I didn't drop the kids off with Harlyn…" She trails off and a tear starts to slide down her cheek, so I wipe it away.

"You were lucky Ro was still following you." He wouldn't have let anything happen to her, and I believe that. He loves her, just like I do.

She turns back to watch the scene in front of us. "I don't give a shit what happens to that bitch," Mica spits before looking back over at us. She has a snarl on her face, and I can see the anger radiating off of her. "I wish he would have gotten a hold of her. She stole him from me." When Tarak turn towards me, I can see the defeat written all over him. He releases her and walks towards me.

He goes to say something, but shakes his head instead. He walks out the door and, when I look back at Mica, she doesn't even look upset. I nod my head to Prez and lead Trix out the door. Closing the door behind us, I walk her a few steps into the hall before she turns and wraps her arms around my neck. I feel her shuddered breath against my neck, and I just hold onto her. Her nails dig into my skin with how hard she's holding on to me.

"Trix, she won't hurt you," I whisper in her ear. Her body shakes and she doesn't say anything. "I won't let whoever is working with her hurt you or the kids. It's us against the world, baby." She nods her head into my neck and I just hold her. I hear footsteps coming closer and, when I look up, I see Tarak standing off to the side. I acknowledge him, but don't release my hold on my girl.

He doesn't say anything, or look annoyed, as he watches us. If anything, he almost looks envious. "I need to talk to Tarak. Stay in sight of the brothers. I'll be out to get you guys soon." I start to pull away from her, but she grips me tighter. Freeing an arm, I grab her chin and force her to look at me. "I love you. I won't let anything happen to the three of you. I swear on my life." I kiss her cheek where another tear is starting to fall and she finally nods her head.

Chapter Nineteen

Watching my Trixibella walk away, I don't focus on anything but her. I hear Tarak's footsteps getting closer, but I don't take my eyes off of her until she's out of sight. "You really do love her," he says. When I look over at him, I can see understanding. He was a lovesick bastard once upon a time.

"I do. I should have cut ties with Tina years ago. Fuck, I should have wifed up Trix the day we started fuckin' on the regular. I've done some shitty things to her, but I won't let this shit go. Your sister knew what she was doing." He sighs and runs his hands over his face.

"I know. I can't fucking believe that she would

even do that shit, especially after she watched what Mary and I went through." He leans back against the wall and I remain silent. I don't even know what to say to him right now. He reaches out and grabs my chin, moving my head to the side to see where he left his mark on my jaw. "Sorry about that," he says, pointing to it, before letting my face go.

"Naw, I get it man. She's your sister. *Fuck*. She's like my sister. Knowing the shit that's going to have to go down because of it isn't something I even want to think about. She's a threat to my family and I can't let that go." I look at him, and I can see the uncertainty written on his face. He still doesn't like the idea of what I'm going to do to her, but my hands are tied.

"I know, in the club's eyes, that she's as good as dead, but isn't there anything you can do?" I don't say anything and, after a few minutes, he just nods. "I get it, man. I really do, but she's still my little sister. The girl I'm supposed to protect."

"She knew what she was doing when she got someone to attack Trix. She admitted to wanting her out of the picture. I'm sorry, Tarak, but there is nothing

I can do or will do to help her." He doesn't say anything else; I can see how much this is affecting him. When the door opens, I see Stavros come out of the room and put the lock in place from the outside. I don't even remember the last time we locked someone in that room.

"What do you want to do, Easy E?" He comes to a stop in front of Tarak and me.

I look over at Tar and then back at Prez. "I want her to confess to the murder of Tina. Let her go through the system. I don't want her blood on my hands." He nods and I continue. "But the fucker that helped her, I want him. I want to make sure he never goes near another woman again." Tarak's hand lands on my shoulder and, when I look over at him, I see the thankful expression on his face.

"That doesn't mean someone on the inside won't take her out, man. That bitch deserves a whole lot more than what she's getting because of what she did to E and his ol' lady." Tarak looks over at me and nods his head. He knows that I'm taking a risk by letting her live.

"If she comes anywhere near me or my family again, I won't hesitate next time. She was family at one time, and I respect the hell out of that and you. That's the only reason I'm doing this. Don't make me regret it."

"I won't, E. Thank you." His voice is choked up and he no longer looks like the guy I've fought beside in the streets. He looks like the brother who would do anything, like selling his soul to the devil, to protect the sister he loves.

"If she doesn't give me the name, I'll have no other choice." He nods his head, and I watch him walk to the door and slowly open it.

"Tarak," she whimpers when she sees him.

"Give him the name. If you so much as lie to me or him, I'll let him kill you." Her eyes swing over to me and I stare at her. She goes to say something smart-assed, I'm sure of it, before she stops herself and walks away from her brother.

"I hope he finds her." Her words are bitter, and I can't hold myself back anymore. I charge at her and push her back against the wall.

Putting my hand on her collarbone, I hold her body against the wall. She kicks at me and screams, but it doesn't do shit. She's skating on thin fuckin' ice with me already, and I won't be afraid to kill her if it means protecting Trix. "If you know what's fuckin' good for you, you will give me the damn name. If anything happens to her, I slit your throat myself." I press down on her arm, and I hear a crack before she starts to scream bloody murder.

Tarak pulls me back and I release her. I watch as she cradles her arm to her body and looks up at me with hate. Good. I hope this bitch hates me by the end of it. She fucked with the wrong person. "Mica," Tarak grits out. "Give us a fucking name."

She shuts her mouth and glares at the both of us. "So help me God bitch, if he touches her…" I trail off when I see her expression. She's got a grin on her face, and I know that this is part of her plan. She wants our attention—*shit.*

I hear a scream coming from somewhere in the clubhouse. Running out of the room, I make my way towards the bar and then I see Trix come out of the hallway. People are rushing around and they are all going the same way I am. She has blood trailing down her face, and she's feeling for the walls. Running over to her, I grab ahold of her and look around the room. I see Blade sitting on the couch with Dex and, when I look for Bexley, I don't see her anywhere.

I run down the hallway towards the bathroom and see blood on the ground and it leads out to where I left Trix standing. Going towards the back door, with my gun drawn, I check outside and see nothing. There isn't a soul outside and I stand quietly to see if I hear anything, but I don't. Making my way back to Trix, I wrap my arms around her.

"What happened?" I ask Trix. She looks up at me with tears in her eyes. "Trix, I need you to tell me what the fuck happened." She tries to get the words out, but nothing comes out. Instead, she just cries. Pulling her to me, I hold her tightly.

"He took her." Her broken, muffled cries make it hard to understand her.

"Who did? Who took our daughter?" I demand. When I pull away from her to look into her eyes, I can see the devastation written all over her face.

"I don't know. I was taking her to the bathroom to clean up her face when I got hit in the side of the head." My eyes scan over her face, and I run my fingers through the blood to find the wound. She pulls away when my fingers make contact with it. "Ow," she whimpers. "We have to find her. Elec, I… I…" I pull her back into my arms and she starts to cry.

"Shh. I'm going to find her." She nods her head against my chest, and I see Stavros come out of the room and right towards me. He gets a look at Trix's bloody head and then looks at me.

"What happened?" His voice is irritated and I don't blame him. I'm just as fuckin' mad, if not more.

"Someone hit her from behind and kidnapped our daughter." He curses before grabs his phone out of his pocket and starts dialing someone's number.

"I need you on the lookout for a missing kid. She's six months old. One of the brothers' kids. Someone just took her from the clubhouse." He listens for a second before he looks over at me. "Dark curly hair, wearing a pink onesie. I can text you a picture, but

I want this shit on the down low. No one needs to know this shit. I pay you fuckers enough money to ensure the privacy this matter needs. If you find the fucker before we do, I want him alive." He doesn't say any more because we all know what he means by his words.

He dials another number and, when the person on the other end answers, I can tell it's his brother. "I need your help again." Before he can start talking again, he makes his way out of the bar and into the hallway. I lead Trix over to where Dex and Blade are sitting. Forcing her to take a seat, I kiss her forehead before making my way to the bathroom to get some wet paper towels to clean the side of her face off.

"Momma, what happened?" Blade points to her face and then crawls into her lap. She hugs him tightly to her body and starts to cry. Blade looks like he's about to cry, too, when I finally reach them. I take the seat the Dex just vacated and Blade looks over at me. "Daddy, momma sad." I nod my head, unable to get any words out. He won't understand what's going on right now, but it doesn't matter. He's sad when his momma is sad and it breaks my fuckin' heart.

Trix turns her head when I ask her to, and I start to wipe the blood from her skin. She looks almost like she's in a state of shock. She doesn't say anything. She just holds onto Blade and cries silently. Blade's eyes watch me the whole time I'm cleaning the blood off of her face. He doesn't ask questions, almost like he knows I won't be able to get the words out. I've had Trix taken once before, and now my six-month-old daughter is missing.

Maybe she was right when she told me that I was slowly ruining her. No, I take that back. I *know* I'm ruining her. I've been doing since the first day I met her.

Walking through the clubhouse, I don't expect to see my Trixibella. She's pissed at me for God knows what reason. It's pretty standard for me to piss her off enough for her to leave me with blue balls that fuckin' kill. If I weren't so

fuckin' hooked on her pussy, I'd be buried deep inside another bitch's cunt. But fuck, I can't bring myself to do it. I'm drawn to Trix even when she pulls fuckin' stunts like she did last night.

When I come up behind her at the bar, my eyes scan over her body and down to her long as fuck legs. She's a fuckin' wet dream if I ever saw one. Her body isn't tiny like most bitches around here; she's got enough curves to keep me begging for more. No other woman holds a candle to my girl.

Reaching out to slide a hand up the back of her skirt, she turns around quickly, hand raised like she's going to slap me. She's fuckin' lucky she doesn't actually slap me because I would have her ass bent over my legs as I spanked her later if she did. "What?" she bites out. My eyes scan over her face, and I can see the anger still radiating from her. She's still pissed from last night, yet she came back for more.

"You know what. You have something to finish." I raise an eyebrow at her and she crosses her arms over her chest, pushing those amazing tits up and together. Fuck.

"I told you last night I was done – " I stop her from saying anything more because she doesn't make the rules, I do.

"No, I make the fuckin' rules here. You are fuckin'

mine. You want to pitch a fit, go for it, but know that I won't let you go until I say you can." Her face pinches into a frown, and I wrap my arm around her waist, pulling her body to mine.

"You're slowly ruining me." Her voice is a soft caress over my ears, and I'm sure she's right about that, but I can't help the way I feel about her. I don't know if its love or not, but it's definitely an addiction that I can't shake even if I wanted to.

When she told me she loved me, I could have said it back, but I didn't. I let her think that she meant nothing more than a fuck to me because I can't handle my feelings for her. She means more to me than my wife or any other woman in my life. She's the excitement in my life, and the vision I see when I lose my eyes.

"Why can't you just let me go?" Her whispered voice is barely audible and, as much as I want to give her the answer she wants, I don't. Instead, I pull her body closer to mine and nip at her earlobe.

"I'll never give you up. You're my drug of choice. I'd rather bring you down into hell with me than let you go. You're the angel that lifts me up when I need to break free from the demons that drag me down." Her forehead presses

down on mine, and our noses touch.

"I'm no angel." Her eyes darken as she wraps her arms around my neck. Her fuck-me heels put her almost at eye level with me. She's standing on her tiptoes, and leaning her amazing fuckin' body against mine.

"Then show me how naughty you can be." She gives me a sexy grin that nearly brings me to my knees. Even when she thinks she better off without me, I show her just how much we need each other.

Chapter Twenty

By the time Stavros comes back into the room, I can't sit still anymore. The only thing on my mind is my baby girl and the fucker who took her. Closing my eyes, I pray that nothing happens to her. Don't think I'd ever forgive myself if something happened to her.

"We need to get information from Mica," he states before making his way towards the room she's being held in.

Walking over to Trix, I kiss the side of her head and lean down to whisper in her ear, "I'll be right back babe." She doesn't even acknowledge me, and I know that she's having a hard time with this. She's probably blaming herself, or me. I'm the reason Mica is in our lives, and the reason she even came up with this plan to get Trix out of my life.

Standing to my full height, I run my hand over Blade's hair before making my way towards the room. When I walk through the door, I see the anger written all over Tarak's face. "How the fuck could you even do that Mica? She's six months old, and you let some bastard fucking take her all because you hate her mother?!" He gets into his sister's face before he says anything else. "You make me fucking sick. You better hope like fucking hell that nothing happens to that little girl."

Walking over to them, I grab the back of her hair, and pull her head back, so she has to look up at me. "I never expected you to be that fuckin' desperate. You fuckin' crossed the line, and there is no way in hell I'll let you get off easy. When I find your little friend, I'll make sure he regrets ever touching a hair on my daughter's head. I'll kill him slowly for even touching Trix and Bexley." I push her head away from me before I continue. "If you give me his name, I'll go easy on you. I'll just put a bullet in you."

Tarak flinches at my words, but I don't pay him any attention. I let him try to get the information I wanted before I took this shit back into my own hands. Now, I'm showing her no mercy. "I'll never tell you shit. I hope he kills her." The crack of a hand hitting skin echoes in the room, and I see her eyes widen when she realizes that it was Tarak who hit her.

Her hand goes to her cheek, and she stares at her brother. "I can't believe—" He cuts her off before she can say the rest of her sentence.

"Don't you dare say you can't believe it. You let a man kidnap a six-month-old child. You have no fuckin' remorse for what you've done. I can't fucking believe we are related. You are sick, and I'm done protecting you." Tarak turns and walks to the door. When he grabs the handle, he turns to look at Stavros and me. "Do what you need to. If you need help getting her back, I'm here." I nod my head and watch him walk out of the room, defeat written all over him.

Standing in front of her, I wait for her to look up at me. Her eyes are no longer angry; they are more hurt than anything. Tarak has always been behind her one hundred percent, no matter what shit she got into. "No one can save you now," I state. Her eyes cut to Stavros and she just shrugs. She's been sitting in here for hours with no other contact other than when we come in and out of the room.

"I don't need saving. You're the one who's going to need it," she spits. Before she can even take another breath, I have her by her throat.

Tightening my fist around her throat, I feel her hands grip my forearm, trying to get me to let her go. "I'm the one who needs it? You should fuckin' think again, bitch. You messed with my family and my little girl. I'll make the rest of your life fuckin' hell. I trusted you." When I loosen my grip a bit, she grins up at me.

"You never gave me a chance. I've been the one you've turned to time after time when those stupid bitches pissed you off." She points to her chest and I just watch her. "When that bitch told you she was pregnant, you ran to me. I've been here for you every time you needed me and, like always, I was cast aside. She forgave you after you told her it wasn't yours, and she still let you fuck her. She's a whore. She's doesn't fucking deserve you! Neither of them did."

I can't fuckin' believe what I'm hearing. Did I call Mica when I had problems in my relationships? Yeah, probably more than I should have, but that doesn't mean anything. It sure as fuck doesn't mean that her and I were together. "You think that just because I called you, we were meant to be together? You're more delusional than I thought. You never even made my radar as more than my best friend's little sister." She scoffs at me, and I can't stop the words from coming out of my mouth. "If I ever fucked you, it would have been to try to get Trix out of my head, but she is so far buried in me that you wouldn't have done shit."

She gasps at my words, and I see the tears fall down her cheeks. "You don't mean that," she whispers.

"You would never be anything to me." I don't show any emotion towards her as she gets up off the chair she is currently sitting in. She comes towards me, and I wait for what she's going to do.

"You love me." Her hand comes to my chest and I just watch her. She goes to hit me, but I grab her wrist and pull her arm behind her back. She struggles against me for a second before she stops.

"You'll never mean a damn thing to me again. Tell me who has my daughter."

Her sad eyes meet my cold ones, and she must see something in them for her to finally talk about my daughter. "He's supposed to get rid of her. I was the distraction." I twist her arm behind her even more and wait for her to continue. She cries out in pain, but I don't give a fuck.

"How is he supposed to get rid of her?" I demand. She flinches at my tone, and I put even more pressure on her arm.

"Sell –"I don't even let her get the last word out before I hit the stupid bitch. A phone rings, and I can't even tell where it's coming from. I'm only focused on Mica, and I am going to fuckin' kill her. If I don't get my daughter back, I'm going to make her suffer.

A hand on my shoulder brings my attention away from the thoughts that are going through my head at the moment. She's fucking dead.

"We need to head out," Stavros says in my ear. I

reluctantly pull away from her, and push her to the ground in front of me.

"If anything happens to Bexley, I will make sure you suffer in the worse possible way." She crawls backwards away from me and towards the wall. Following Stavros out the door, I think about getting my daughter back. It better be the fuckin' reason that he's even pulling me out of that room.

"I got a lead. We need to move," he states before I can ask him *what the fuck*.

"Where?" I demand as we make our way through the clubhouse.

"Thirty miles outside of town. A buy is about to go down." A black sedan pulls into the parking lot just as we walk out the doors. The door opens, and we see Nikolai pulling a bag out of the backseat. He hands it to Stavros, and he nods his head to me. A few of the others are trailing behind us, including Romeo.

"Who is staying to watch Mica?" I ask.

"Mirror is making sure that bitch doesn't leave the room, and Dex has your girl and son. The prospects are staying behind, too, just in case." I nod my head and grab the other bag that Nikolai shoves at us. "You following?" he asks Nikolai.

"Yeah. I'll be where you need. I have a car seat, too." I slap Nikolai on the back and walk over to the others. I watch Tarak make his way to Nikolai and say something to him. They both get into Niko's car. Putting the bag into my saddlebags, I straddle my Harley and crank the engine. The roar of my engine and the men around me's engines roar loud. On Prez's signal, we take off towards the meeting place that he was tipped off about.

The only thought on my mind the whole fuckin' ride is getting my daughter back. If I don't get her back, I don't know what I'm going to do. Trix will be devastated. Fuck, so will I. *Fuck that,* there is no way that I'm not bringing my little girl home with me.

The ride feels like it takes fuckin' forever, but when we get about a mile away, we pull off the road. Stavros and I both grab the stuff from our saddlebags and start to hand out the AR15's that Nikolai brought us. He pulls in behind us and I toss the empty bag back at him. He catches it and looks us all over before pulling out his phone and pressing it to his ear.

"Yeah?" He looks down at the ground, and I can feel my anger rising with every second that we are not heading towards the meet to kill the fuckers who have my daughter.

"Why the fuck are we just standing here?" I growl, when nothing happens. Stavros looks over at Nikolai, but doesn't answer me. They both look at each other, and then Stavros turns back to me.

"Niko is dealing with it. We go on his word and not a second sooner." I push past him and make my way to my bike, but he stops me with a few words. "If it's not timed right, they'll take her underground." I freeze, and look over my shoulder at my brothers. They all have grim expressions on their faces.

Half of these fuckers have kids and/or ol' ladies, but none of them move from their current places. They wait for word to move and I hate it. I fuckin' hate that we are standing here with our thumbs up our asses while my little girl is just a mile away with people she doesn't know. Who the fuck knows what they've done to her since they've had her?

Fuck. My mind is racing, and the only thing I can think of at the moment is Bex and leaving Trix without a word. She's going to fuckin' hate me even more than before. Closing my eyes, I run my hands over my face and take a deep breath.

"You sure?" The words bring me out of my head and I look over at Nikolai. He's talking in hushed tones to someone on the phone. My phone buzzes in my pocket and, when I pull it out, I see three angels smiling back at me. Trix's contact picture is staring at me and, as much as I want to let it go to voicemail, I hit the ANSWER button and put my phone to my ear.

"Elec…" Her voice breaks, and it tears at me.

"Yeah, baby?" I finally choke out.

"Please bring her back." I can picture the way her lip trembles as she says the words. "Be safe, but bring our little girl home." Running my fingers through my hair, I slick it back and tug on the ends.

"I won't come back without her," I finally say around the lump in my throat. I hear her intake of breath and the sob that follows.

"I should have taken someone with me to—" I

cut her off because this shit isn't her fault, and I don't want her blaming herself.

"You didn't do anything wrong. Don't think that. I will get our girl back, and I'll bring her home where she belongs." I can hear her cries over the line, and I just pray to God that Niko's intel is right about this location.

"Got it. Ten minutes," Niko says from behind me. I turn to look at him and he has that deadly look on his face that he got when we went in after Stavros and Harlyn.

"Baby, I need to go. I'll call you when I have our girl." I hear her sharp intake of breath and Blade's voice in the background.

"Please come back to me. Both of you. I love you, Elec." My heart skips a beat and my throat goes dry.

"We will. Love you, angel." I hang up before she can say anything else. Part of me isn't even sure that I could take anything else. She doesn't deserve the heartbreak that can be part of this outcome, and I'll do what it takes to make sure she gets the happy ending she's always wanted.

Pocketing my phone, I make my way towards Stavros and Niko. They are talking quietly to each other and, when they pull apart, I see the look on Stavros' face. He's pissed and part of me is glad that he is. A pissed Stavros gets shit done and takes no prisoners.

"Let's move. Bikes stay here. We don't want them to know we are coming. Meet starts in eight minutes." We make our way towards the meet location. My heart is pounding with anger and adrenaline. My finger is itching to pull the trigger on the AR15 that is currently in my right hand. I have a knife in my holster on my hip, and I have a Glock in the back of my jeans.

When we get to the site, I see a black SUV idling next to an abandoned building. We watch as another dark SUV comes to a stop next to the first one. A man steps out of the black SUV and he looks familiar. I don't know where the fuck I've seen him before, but I know that I have.

A man steps out of the dark grey SUV, and then they both come to a stop in front of the vehicles. My eyes never leave them as they shake hands. Watching them talk to each other, I get a feeling in my gut that she's not here. If she were, wouldn't they have brought her out by now?

Chapter Twenty-One

Another door opens and a briefcase is brought out. My feet start to move, but Stavros holds me back. His hand on my arm is the only reason I'm not walking right towards them right now.

Once the briefcase is opened, and the first guy looks it over, he nods his head and another door opens, showing me my little girl. Her hair is dyed a dirty blonde color, and she's no longer wearing the pink onesie that Trix put her in this morning. They must have changed her appearance so none of us would recognize her if we saw her.

I pull away from Stavros, and start to make my way towards them. The rest of the guys follow behind me, but I don't hear a sound. My only thought is getting my daughter back. Her now dirty blonde head turns towards me and, when she sees me, she squeals, "Dada!" Her high pitch squeal sends all the heads in our direction and the woman holding her tries to get back into the car.

Gunshots erupt, and I run straight for the bitch that has my daughter, while the others go after the men that are now shooting at us. More men appear out of nowhere and join in on the gunfire. The man from in front of the SUV tries to get into the car, but I put a bullet in his knee causing him to scream out in pain and drop to the ground. Someone else comes up behind me and puts me in a chokehold.

I can feel my throat starting to close, and I'm having a hard time breathing. Taking the gun in my hand, I position it behind me and pull the trigger. When he releases me, I almost fall to my knees, gasping for breath. When I can finally get up, I run over to the door and open it. The woman looks freaked the fuck out, and my little girl has big tears running down her face.

"Bex," I whisper. I grab her out of the bitch's hands and she tries to attack me. Grabbing the bitch's throat, I squeeze and her eyes widen. "You touch my daughter again, and I'll be sure to put a bullet between your eyes." She nods her head, hands digging into my forearm.

Bex puts her head on my shoulder, and I just hug her tighter to me. The fucker I shot in the knee takes the door and swings it at me. I move just in time to get Bex out of the way of it. The door hits me in the back and knocks me off balance enough for the other fucker to kick my knee out from under me, causing me to hit the ground. I barely have enough time to turn my shoulder to protect Bexley from the fall. A gunshot goes off next to me, and I feel the bullet as it slices through my skin.

I grit my teeth in pain and another shot goes off behind me. I cover Bexley with my body and turn my gun and shoot the fucker that shot me. The bullet goes between his eyes and blood splatters all over us. The bitch in the car starts to scream just as another bullet nicks my shoulder. Bex is full on screaming her head off, and I try to protect her as much as I can. The fucker steps on my hand with the gun until I release it and he kicks it out of reach.

"You'll fucking die for killing my brother," the dickhead behind me says. I close my eyes and shield my daughter's body with mine.

I hear the gunshot go off and the only thing running through my head is making sure she lives through this. If dying to protect my daughter is what I have to sacrifice, then I'll gladly do it. Another shot goes off at the same time, and I feel the burn as the bullet goes into my shoulder. The woman in the car starts to scream, and I fall to the ground. Bexley's small hands grab at my face and she cries louder.

Someone comes running towards us and, when the woman tries to take Bex from me, I hold on tighter. A shadow comes over me and gets in between me and the bitch trying to take Bex. "Get the fuck away from him or I won't hesitate to put a bullet in you, too," Romeo's voice grates out from above me. A hand pushes against my back, and I hear something hit the ground.

"He going to live?" I think it's Stavros this time.

"I can hear you, fuckhead," I groan. Romeo helps me up enough to get Bex. He pulls her out from under me, and I feel like I can finally breathe a little. My back is on fire, but that doesn't keep me from my daughter. She cries harder when Romeo has her. Tarak helps me sit against the car, and Romeo hands Bex back to me. She grips me tight in her little hands, and I just breathe in her baby scent.

"Who the hell are you?" the bitch next to me asks.

"I'm her father." I hear her gasp and, when I look up at her, I see her wide eyes. "Your friend there kidnapped her." I nod to the dead body of the fucker who was driving the car. Nikolai comes walking towards us, and I can feel the blood dripping down my back into the back of my jeans.

"We need to get you checked out, E. I put some plastic down in my back seat. Tarak, can you ride his bike back?" Tar nods his head and motions to the woman.

"What are we doing about the bitch?" Her face

pales and Niko shrugs his shoulders.

"We can kill her like the rest of these fuckers that were involved in this child trafficking ring or we can take her with us." Stavros narrows his eyes at his brother. I don't say a word because they already know my opinion. Moving slightly, I try to pull my phone out of my pocket. I fail the first three times to grab it, so Tarak reaches into my pocket to grab it for me.

When he looks at the screen, he shows it to me and I see the crack. He hits the button to turn it on, but it does nothing. Fuck. Stavros tosses me his phone, so I turn the camera on and snap a photo of me and Bexley. Pulling up his text messages, I attach it to a message to Trix. Hitting the send button, I hand him his phone back and bury my face into her small neck.

She's no longer crying and I thank fuck for that. I'm not good with a crying baby, that's more Trix's expertise. Every time one of the kid's cries, she does something that brings a smile to their face a few minutes later. Cradling my little one against me, I thank God for protecting her.

"Let's get the fuck out of here and get you to a

doctor. We need to get her checked out, too." I nod my head and I reach a hand out. Tarak pulls me to my feet, but it's not without a few fuckin' pains in my back and shoulder. I can feel more blood pumping out of the holes with the strain of being pulled up, but I'm not putting her down.

Niko's car pulls up, and he walks over to the back door and opens it for me. I take a seat on the plastic and situate Bexley on my lap. Niko shuts the door, and I roll down the window. "Tar!" I shout. He comes over to me and leans into the window. "Keys." He nods his head and goes to walk away, but I stop him. "Thank you. Thank you for helping me get Bex back."

"You know I'd do anything for you. You're my brother." I look down for a minute when I think about the shit that we are going back to. We still have to deal with Mica and the shit she pulled.

"I get it if you hate me after we get back, but I have to do what I have to do." He nods, but doesn't say a word. He turns to walk away again and, this time, I let him. I don't bother stopping him.

When the car takes off into the night, I close my eyes and lean back in the seat. Feeling her heartbeat against my chest calms me like only her mother does. All the shit from today disappears and the only thing I can see is my family. I can't wait to get home to my girl and son.

I can feel every bump in the damn road as we drive over them, and I grit my teeth to keep from swearing. Bex's hand never loosens her grip on my tee shirt. Closing my eyes, I drift off to sleep.

Looking at Trix, I feel my heart stop. She's fuckin' beautiful even with her hair piled on the top of her head. She has no makeup on, and my tee shirt that she's wearing is cut down the sides for the gym. She rocks it without a care in the world, and I love that I'm the one who gets to see her like this. She doesn't notice me come in the room. She's currently cleaning her apartment with music blasting. Her barely there panties peek out under my shirt and I can't help but smile.

Walking closer to her, I grab her around the waist and pull her back into my front. Her hand goes to her chest and she squeals. She turns in my arms and wraps her arms around my neck. "You scared the crap out of me, asshole." She grins up at me, and I place a kiss on her mouth.

"Maybe you should turn that shit down, so you can hear when people come in your apartment." I run my hands through the sides of her hair.

"You're the only one with a key. I know the door was locked," she whispers against my lips before she closes the distance between us. I claim her mouth roughly and her moan fills my ears.

"Yeah, but baby there's fuckin' crazy people around here. I don't want anything to happen to you." I place a kiss to her jaw and she rolls her eyes at me.

"No one is going to want to hurt me. I'm sure they know they'd have to deal with you, and we all know that isn't something people want to do." I grab her ass cheeks and give them a squeeze.

"Not everyone knows your mine. They may not care either." She eyes me for a second before she says anything else.

"It almost sounds like you worry about me… Does

this mean you actually care about what happens to me?" She's got a small grin tugging at the corner of her mouth.

"You know damn well I care about you, angel."

"You never say it. You've never once told me how you felt about me." I frown at her words and try to think back to if she's right. Nothing comes to mind and I pick her up. Her legs wrap around my waist. Walking us towards her room, I run my mouth down her neck. "You can't think of a single time, can you?" she asks, running her fingers through the short Mohawk that my hair is typically styled in. Her fingers run across the shaved sides of my head and, fuck, it feels good.

"Say it." Her voice has a hint of playfulness, but I know that she's trying to get me to say three words to her. Three words that I refuse to tell anyone, including my wife. "Do you tell your wife you love her?" It's almost like she can read my mind sometimes.

"No, but then again, I don't love that bitch." Her eyebrow raises and I ignore it.

"If you don't love her, then why marry her?" We typically don't talk about Tina because personally, when I'm inside Trix, I don't want to think about anyone but her.

"Because I was young and fuckin' dumb. I was

thinking with my dick." She snorts at my answer.

"I'm pretty sure you are still thinking with your dick. How else would you end up in bed with someone other than your wife?" She's got a smirk on her face and, as much as I want to tell her she's wrong, I don't. Part of it is true, but there's more that I don't tell her.

I don't tell her that she takes my breath away with just one smile, and that I knew I was a goner the night I fuckin' met her. I don't tell her that six hours was all it took for her to put me under her spell. "With you, it's different." A real smile breaks out across her face, and she grabs my face with her hands.

"How so?" I press my hips into her body and her hands run down the length of my back. Her cold hands snake under my tee shirt and cut.

"Because." I nip at her chin before I continue. "You are the sexiest woman I've ever seen." I move my mouth down her neck to her chest. "I love the way you feel wrapped around me." I pull the shirt to the side and suck a nipple into my mouth. "I especially love the sounds you make when I take you." I bite down gently on her nipple and she moans out my name.

"Elec." Her legs lock around my waist and her bare

feet dig into my ass. "Oh, God," she whimpers. My hand slides down her body to her panties. Pushing them to the side, I sink a finger inside of her. Her back arches, and I start to pump my finger in and out of her until she's begging me for more.

Undoing my jeans, I slide them off and kick my boots off with them. Her hands make quick work of my cut and tee shirt. Lining myself up with her sweet cunt, I slam into her in one hard stroke. Her hands grip my back and I can feel her nails digging into my skin.

I fuck her long and hard until we are both panting, and I'm ready to blow my load inside of her. I thrust into her a few more times before her eyes roll in the back of her head and she's yelling my name. I pump my hips a few more times before I'm coming inside of her. Collapsing on top of her, I huff out a breath and let my body weight push her deeper into the mattress. Her fingers reach up and she starts to run her fingers through my hair again like she always does.

"You need to shave the sides again," she says, sounding a little breathy still.

"I'm waiting on you, babe." My breath fans against her chest and she just giggles.

"I'm not your hairstylist."

"No, but you're my girl and I already know if I let Tina do it, you'll bitch at me for it." When I look at her face, I see the frown marring her beautiful features. Tina's been cutting my hair since we were sixteen.

"I don't bitch." She pouts out her bottom lip. Leaning forward, I take her bottom lip into my mouth and suck it into my mouth.

"You do too, but I find it sexy as hell. It shows me that I mean something to you." Her lips curve into a grin, and she wraps her arms around my neck.

"That's because you do." I can see the words on the tip of her tongue, but she doesn't let them fall from her lips. She loves me. Shit. I don't know how to handle love.

"Come on, cut my hair, so you can run your fingers along my scalp." She shakes her head at me, but waits for me to roll off of her so she can get up and get the clippers.

Chapter Twenty-Two

I'm jolted awake from something being drug into my back. My fingers clench when I look up to see the doc standing over me with tweezers in her hand. She never does shit gently, almost like she like to inflict pain on us. "Nice to see you finally awake," she muses.

I flip her the bird and mutter under my breath as she pulls something out of the wound. "Fuck. Why the fuck couldn't you put me out before you started?" I bitch. She just grins at me and starts to dig again.

"Because where is the fun in that? Plus, I'm almost done. You've been out for the last two hours." I rise up on my forearms and look around the room. She's working on my lower back, and I see Tarak standing off to the side of the room. He nods at me, but doesn't say anything.

My mind starts to remember why the fuck I got shot and when I look back at the doc it's almost like she already knows what I'm going to ask before I do. "How's my daughter?" I finally push the words past my lips. Part of me is afraid that we got there too late and someone hurt her.

"I did a full exam before I started working on you." I hold my breath as I wait for what she found. "Your daughter is in perfect health, has no signs of anything being done to her, and I've already talked to your ol' lady about her health, too." I blow out the breath I was holding. Relief rushes through my veins and my erratic beating heart takes it down a notch.

"Thank Christ." I murmur before I lay back down on the table as she finishes working on me.

"They are both beautiful, E," she states before she pushes the needle through my skin. I suck in a breath and grit my teeth against the pain.

"Is that your bedside manner? Complimenting me about my ol' lady and daughter before shoving that fuckin' needle in me?" I look over my shoulder at her and see the smirk on her face.

"Next time, I can tell you how much I love when I get you to take your shirt off instead… if that works better?" She grins at me, and I hear Tarak stifling a laugh from the corner.

"Naw, I'd rather you talk about them," I finally say before putting my head back down on the table I'm fuckin' sprawled out on. I focus on my family's faces as she continues to stitch me up. It takes some of the pain away, but not all of it. I swear she's trying to get me to react with each poke of the needle.

The door opens a few minutes later, and I see long fuckable legs walking towards the table. As my eyes roam up her body, I see the tattoo on her thigh, the same one that is tattooed on my arm. When my eyes hit her face, I can see the tears in her eyes and the wet streaks that trail down her cheeks. "Elec," she whimpers. The doc pats my leg, telling me she's done. I try to slide off the table, but I grunt out in pain. Before I can move another inch, Tarak is helping me stand. She tentatively walks closer to me, but doesn't reach out to touch me like she normally does. Her eyes scan over every inch of my naked upper body, and then down to my jeans that are covered in blood still.

Tarak lets me go when I get my footing back, and I take a few small steps that tug at the new stitches. Using my good arm, I reach out and wrap my hand around the back of her neck, pulling her to me. Her small hands land on my chest and I pull her even closer. Her eyes widen and she pushes me away from her, but a growl rumbles from deep down in my chest and she relents.

Her face buries in my chest, and I can feel her body rack with sobs. Doc gives me a small wave of her hand before her and Tarak leave the room. I stand there holding Trix until she can't cry anymore. I have no idea what is running through her head right now. When the pain in my back becomes too much, I lead her towards the small couch that takes up part of the small room. I slowly lower my body to the couch and her eyes never leave my body.

When I lean back against the couch, it pulls a little at my stitches, but I grit my teeth through the pain. "Elec, are you okay?" Her voice is low and concerned. I hate when she worries about me but, at the same time, it makes me hard. She's the only woman in my life to ever be concerned with me getting hurt or not making it back alive.

"I'll be fine. The doc stitched me up. How's our girl?" She takes a seat next to me and curls her feet under her body. She's facing me so I can see all the emotions as they cross over her beautiful face. She's still upset and scared, but I don't think those will ever change for as long as she's with me. This life isn't hearts and rainbows. It is death and violence. She's the angel to my bastard self, and I hate for her to be messed up in my shit life, but I can't let her go either. I've already tried and that blew the fuck up in my face.

I pull her towards me and her face rests on my chest. "She's okay," she whispers against my bare skin. My hands go to her hair, and I tangle them into the soft red strands. Her breath is warm as it floats over my skin, and the only thing I can think of is her and the kids.

When her tears finally dry, I pull her over me to

straddle my lap. She tries to keep most of her weight off of me, but I pull her down on top of me. "I'm going to be fine, babe. I need your mouth, though." She watches me hesitantly for a second before she brings her mouth down on mine. Closing my eyes, I drown myself in her: her taste, her smell, and just the fact that I know she's mine.

"I was so scared I'd lost you," she finally says when she pulls away from me. Her bottom lip trembles.

"You won't lose me, angel," I whisper. My hand cups the back of her neck and I pull her forehead down to mine. "I won't lie and say that you almost didn't, but I would have given my life for hers." She sucks in a deep breath, and more tears fall from her eyes. It tears me up inside to see the heartbreak and uncertainty in her eyes. She's scared she almost lost us both. Fuck if I wasn't scared as all hell at the thought of dying. I haven't had enough time with any of them. I haven't had a chance to be a better father to them, and I sure as hell haven't had enough time to prove to her that I'm worthy of her love.

"I love you so much," she chokes out. Her fingers grab the top of my hair and she pulls my head back. Looking into her eyes, I see the love she has for me as well as the fear of not getting to have me longer than she already has.

"I love you too, babe." I put pressure on her neck until her lips come down onto mine. My hands slide down her back and to her ass. Just as I squeeze her ass cheeks, the door opens and in come two of the lights of my life. Bex is crawling towards us, and Blade is walking slowly behind her. He's encouraging her to come towards us and, when she gets to the couch, she pulls herself up and grabs onto my leg. Trix turns in my lap and shifts most of her weight off of me, making room for both of the kids to take a seat on me.

She pulls Bexley up and into my lap, and Blade gingerly makes his way to me. He slowly climbs on the couch and sits next to me, almost like he's going to hurt me. Grabbing his small body, I haul him into my lap next to Bex and his eyes shoot over to his momma.

"I no want hurt uoh daddy," he says quietly.

"I'm tough, kid. I'll be fine," I say, smiling down

at him. He looks over at Stavros standing in the doorway, and I watch as Stavros nods to him. Even as a kid, he respects Stavros. When his eyes meet me, I give him a smile and he slowly comes closer.

"Daddy." His voice is soft and quiet.

"Yeah, buddy?" I ask when he doesn't continue.

"You safed sissy." The door to the room closes, and I can feel my resolve start to disappear. I was going to stay strong for them even with the pain and fear I felt, but watching the trembling bottom lip of my son brings me to my knees.

"I did, but I would have done it for you, your sissy, *and* your momma if I had to." He nods his head up and down before pressing his face into my neck. He wraps his arms around me and squeezes my neck tightly.

"Luv you daddy." I wrap my arm around him tightly and hold him close to me.

"Love you more, buddy," I whisper. Bex climbs on me and puts her head against my chest, too, mimicking her brother. I hold them both close to me and, when I look up at my Trixibella, I can see the tears in her eyes. She leans closer and wraps her arms around all of us.

Walking out of my room, where I left the three of them sleeping, I make my way towards the bar. After the fuckin' night I had, I think I deserve a drink. When I reach the bar, the prospect eyes me before he puts a glass down and pours some bourbon into it. "Glad to see you alive." He tips his head in respect, and I shoot back the bourbon before I say anything.

"Yeah. We deal with her yet?" I ask to my left. When his eyes turn to me, I watch him.

"No, waiting on you," Stavros says in a deadly tone. "Didn't think you'd appreciate the party starting without you." I nod my head and motion to the kid to pour me another glass. This time, when he pours the amber liquid into the glass, he leaves the bottle behind and goes to the back to give Prez and me some privacy.

"I can't believe I was stupid enough to trust

her." I shake my head and take a swallow of the bourbon, letting the burn make its way through my chest.

"Do you think that it's over once we deal with her? Or are there more people involved?" I ask. When I look over at him, I can't make out his expression. Boots come up behind us and, when I turn around, I see Romeo come walking up. He takes the stool next to Stavros, and leans over the bar to grab a glass. He reaches across Stavros to grab the bottle in front of me, and pours a healthy amount into the glass. He passes the bottle back, and I pour more into my glass.

Before I can take another gulp, hands run down my sides and then come to rest on my abs. I see the look on Ro's face from the corner of my eye, and I know that it's Trix. Her tits press against my back and I can feel her breath on my neck. "Is this nightmare over with yet?" Her voice is stronger than earlier and part of me is glad. My girl has always been strong, and she was starting to worry me with all the crying she was doing when I first saw her after the stitches.

"No. I still need to deal with Mica," I grunt out.

It makes me sick to think that I have to kill my best friend's little sister. It's not something that I want to do, but she endangered my family so I have no choice now.

"Are you going...?" She trails off and looks over at the two sitting beside me. She doesn't need me to answer her because she already knows what the outcome is going to be. She reaches around me, grabs my glass off the bar, and downs it all in a few gulps. Wrapping my arm around her waist, I watch her close her eyes as the liquid burns going down. She makes a cute face that tells me she doesn't like the taste of what I'm drinking and shakes her head a little.

Grabbing the back of her head, I pull her mouth down on mine and claim it. Part of it is to make sure that Ro knows that he isn't getting what's mine again, but the other part is to show her that she's mine. When I finally release her, she is out of breath and the look on Ro's face is murderous.

I shove my hand in the back of her pajama shorts, my hand grips her ass and I feel her tense as she remembers who we are in front of. My fingers gently move along her ass crack and the tension starts to fade little by little. She's not big on letting me stick my dick in her ass, but the way her body is responding, I just might have a chance to get inside of her tight little hole.

I can feel her wetness and she moves a little as my finger starts to slowly move closer to her sweet cunt. My finger dips into her wetness, and her breathy sigh tells me all I need to know. She's horny and wants my dick. It might even be the original reason she got out of bed to find me. Sliding my fingers through her wetness, I work her up a little before I remove my fingers from her and pull them out of her shorts. She huffs out, and I can hear the laughter that Stavros is trying to muffle.

Turning my chair towards her, I put my fingers in my mouth and suck her juices off of them. Her eyes darken with lust as she watches me. My dick is pressing hard against my zipper, but I have shit to do, so fuckin' her right now isn't going to happen, as much as I want it too. It's been too damn long since I've been inside of her.

Pulling her head down to mine, I whisper against her lips. "Once I deal with her, I'll come back to the room to fuck you." She nods her head in agreement, and a glass slams against the bar. Her eyes meet his over my shoulder, and I can see the pain in hers as she watches him. She's hurting because he's affected by seeing us together.

My arm around her back tightens and her hands rest on my waist. "He'll be fine. He'll get over it after some time." She's the only one who can hear my words. Her grip on me tightens with my words and, when they finally break their staring contest, she turns her attention back to me.

"I love you," I say, loud enough for him to hear. Her eyes soften, and a smile forms on her lips.

"I love you, too. Come back to bed soon." I lean into her and kiss her. The sound of glass breaking pulls her away from me. Good, I'm fuckin' glad that prick is jealous. I fuckin' hope this shit eats away at him. He fuckin' deserves it after trying to steal my girl from me.

Chapter Twenty-Three

The sound of our boots walking towards the door is the only thing that I can focus on right now. All thoughts of my Trixibella, Blade, and Bexley are pushed into the back of my mind. I won't ever taint them with this. The blood on my hands is my own, and it will never touch any of them. The moment Romeo opens the door to the room, I see Mica's head pop up. Her eyes scan over both Stavros and Romeo before they land on me.

"What more are you going to do to me? You think I'm scared of your stupid asses?" A grin appears on my face as I stalk towards her. The door shuts behind me, and the loud bang it makes causes her to jump. She is fuckin' scared of us. She knows more about this club than most outsiders, and that's only because she's our lawyer.

She's gotten a few of us off with just slaps on the wrists before even though we were guiltier than the next man. Spilling her blood won't make shit better, but it will ensure that she never has the chance to go after my family again. She's delusional if she thinks that I'd ever let the mother of my children go to prison for a crime she didn't commit.

I walk around her, and she tries to fight against the ropes that bind her in place. Pulling my knife out of my holder, I run it along her skin. Her eyes widen a fraction and before most could tell she was frightened, they return to the darkness I've seen over the last two days. She isn't the girl I grew up with, and she sure as hell doesn't deserve to live after today.

"Just kill me already," she demands. She doesn't understand that we don't take orders; we give them. No woman is going to tell us what to do and when to fuckin' do it.

"Naw, I'd rather take my time with you. After

all, you did let some fuckin' psychopath kidnap my daughter." I put the knife to her throat, and a whimper falls from her lips. The grin spreads across my lips, and I can feel my hate and anger towards her take over my senses.

"E." Her breathing is ragged and her eyes are wide.

"Don't 'E' me. My daughter could have been sold. That shit isn't ever going to be okay with me. You fucked with the wrong man." She struggles to pull her head away from where I have the knife against her throat. Little red rivers run down her skin as she fights me. Each nick in her skin brings a whimper from her mouth.

"You apparently don't understand not to fuck with the Draconic Crimson," Stavros says from behind me. "I thought that, after being our lawyer and knowing what you know about us, you would keep your fuckin' ass from making the stupidest mother fuckin' decision of your life." Her eyes cut to Romeo, and I can see her trying to get him to help her. Although I wouldn't put it past the fucker, I watch their exchange. They watch each other almost like they are communicating without the words.

Stavros notices it, too, and walks over to Romeo. I watch him whisper something in his ear before his eyes flash to mine. I don't give a fuck what Ro and Mica had going with each other, but it ends now. If I find out he had anything to do with the kidnapping of my daughter, I'll fuckin' kill the bastard.

Stavros grabs the knife from my hand and hands it over to Ro. Ro's eyes harden, and he looks over at Mica and then at me before he takes a step closer to her. He puts the knife to her neck, and I watch her eyes widen in surprise. There is something fuckin' going on between the two of them, I just need to figure out what the fuck it was.

"Please don't," she whimpers when he pushes the blade into her skin. I can see the indent its leaving before it actually slices through her skin. "I promise I won't do anything against the club again." Her voice is turning hoarse as she begs for her life.

"You really think that the shit you caused is gonna be forgiven just because you're begging for your life?" I bark out in laughter. Her attention turns to me, and she gives me a dirty look, before looking back to Romeo.

"Please," she whispers to him.

Stavros nods his head to Romeo and I watch as he presses the knife deeper into her skin causing her to cry out in pain. As much as I want to be the one to kill the fuckin' bitch, I know what Stavros is doing. He's testing Ro's loyalty to us. He must suspect the same thing I do, or he would've let me do the fuckin' honors.

"Anyone else involved in this shit with you?" I demand before he kills her.

"Fuck you," she spits at me, struggling against the grip Romeo has on her. She only causes the knife to dig deeper into her skin. She screams out bloody murder, but it doesn't get Ro to remove the knife from her throat.

"Give him the answer he wants," Ro growls. Her eyes widen at his tone before she looks back at him.

"No." She refuses to look at me again and, instead of waiting for her to answer me, I walk over to her and grab the phone out of her bag that is sitting on the floor from when we brought her ass in here. I should have looked at it sooner, but I had other fuckin' things on my mind.

When I turn the screen on, I go to her call log and scan through the numbers. A couple I recognize as my own and Tarak's. I come across another one that she's called a few times over the last few days. Hitting the call button, I put the phone to my ear and wait for someone to pick it up.

Before the call goes to the voicemail, a gravelly voice answers. "I told you not to call me again, you stupid bitch," the voice barks out.

I put the phone on speaker for her and Ro forces her to say something. "They know it all," she chokes out.

"What the fuck is wrong with you?" I can hear the deep breath that the voice takes before he continues. "I told you to stay away from the kid, and you just couldn't help yourself. You wouldn't leave the bitch alone. I hope they fucking kill you. It keeps my hands clean of your bullshit. Good luck." The line goes dead, and she looks up at me.

"Who was that?" I demand. She rolls her eyes at me, and I take the knife that Stavros has in his hand and walk closer to her. I run the blade down her chest and stop at her abdomen. I start to press the blade into her skin and watch her face. As the knife slowly starts to separate her skin, she screams out. When I get the blade half way into her, she begs me to stop.

"I'll tell you everything," she whimpers. I leave the knife right where it is because I know her better than that. She will say anything to get what she wants.

"Start fuckin' talking," I bite out.

"He's a guy from our past. He wants to ruin you," she rushes out. I put a little more pressure on the knife and she starts to talk again. "You remember the guys that Tarak got involved with?" I frown and look back at Stavros. He shrugs and starts to make his way towards the door. "He knows that you are the one who got Tar out of the mess he found himself in when we were younger. You killed his brother, and he wants to make you pay." She sucks in a harsh breath and her breathing starts to get shallow.

I pull the blade out of her stomach and tears

start to fall down her face. "He found me, and threatened to kill me, if I didn't help him."

"You didn't have to help him," I growl. "You could have fuckin' came to me and I would have fuckin' protected you."

A bitter laugh escapes from her lips and she shakes her head. "No, I couldn't. You were too consumed by that bitch and your son," she sneers. "You couldn't see what was right in front of you. She messes up your head and you let her. I hope he kills her like he has planned." I look at Romeo and the murderous look on his face is probably the same one on mine.

Having him still care about her works to my benefit. He won't let anything happen to her and he'll protect my kids because of how he feels for her.

"She never deserved you. She's a whore who's fucked all your brothers. How can you trust a bitch who didn't mind sleeping with them?"

"When we got serious, she stopped. I knew what she was before I got involved with her, and it doesn't change how I feel about her. She saved me; something you could never compete with." She frowns, and I nod to Romeo to finish the job. We now have the rest of the info we need to find the last piece of this fuckin' puzzle. Now, I need to talk to Tarak.

I watch as Ro slits her throat, and the blood sprays on my shirt and jeans. Blood covers his hands and I can see a cloud of sadness written all over her face. She gurgles up blood and, in minutes, her head lolls to the side, her eyes still widen open.

"Were you fuckin' her?" I ask. I don't get what their relationship consists of, but I want to know.

"I made a few mistakes. When Trix and I fought and I left after I found out about not being Bex's father, I ran into Mica at the bar. One thing led to another, and I went home with her." He shakes his head and huffs out. "It was fuckin' stupid and it only made shit worse. I never told her what happened, and I'm sure you are going to tell her just to spite me." He wipes his bloody hand on his jeans before he runs it through his hair. He pulls out the bun thing in his hair, and runs his finger through it.

"I won't tell her, but, in exchange, I want you to

stay away. I don't mind you two being friends, but I'm done letting you pine over my woman." He doesn't say anything as he watches me. "I need help keeping her safe until we find that fucker that is involved. Her life is on the line, and I'll do anything to make sure nothing happens to her."

"You have my word," he states finally. "I've got your back." I reach a hand out, he takes it in his, and we shake on it. One thing about brotherhood is that we always have each other's backs even if there is shit between us. I don't mind keeping his secret, but if he continues to pursue her, I won't hesitate to tell her the truth.

The door opens behind us, and Stavros comes in, Tarak a few steps behind him. Tarak's eyes scan over the scene in front of him, and I watch as he tries to get a hold of his emotions. When he looks at Romeo, his eyes scan over the blood that still covers his hands. His eyes scan over me next, and he sees her blood spilled on me as well.

"What do you remember about the time I helped you out of trouble?" He doesn't say anything at first, but I can tell when the memories hit him.

"The first time you got blood on your hands." I nod in agreement because it's true. Before that, I was a semi good kid. Yeah, we fucked around and got into trouble more times than not, but it was the first time I killed someone. I did it to protect Tarak, and I ended up getting off with self-defense. He started running with the wrong crowd, and I tried like hell to bring him back, but it was no use until that happened.

"His brother is the one behind this shit." Tarak's eyes widen, and I watch his face pale.

"She got involved with him? No fucking way. You and I both know she wouldn't turn her back on us," he states with authority.

"She admitted to it," Romeo says. Tarak's eyes shoot over to him and he shakes his head. "We heard the phone call she made to him, and he told her that he hoped we would take care of her so he wouldn't get his hands dirty."

He continues to shake his head at the information. "No. She wouldn't turn on us… Would she?"

"She wanted Trix out of the picture. She wanted to take her place in my life, and it made her do stupid shit. That fucker has plans for my girl, and there is no fuckin' way that I'll let him touch her. He wants to take her, so I know what it feels like. I am the one who took his brother away from him, and now he's coming to take her. That shit isn't happening."

I will go to fuckin' war alone if I have to. I won't let my past touch her again. She doesn't deserve that shit. My hell and demons won't come near her. I may be a bastard, but I protect what's mine no matter the cost.

Chapter Twenty-Four

"Ro, get the prospects to clean this shit up. You and E need to get cleaned up. Church is in an hour. Tarak, we are going to need some info from you, so I'd like for you to sit in." Tarak doesn't say no to him, and I know it's more of a respect thing than anything else. He's probably just as pissed at Stavros as he is at Ro and I.

We all walk our separate ways when Stavros dismisses us. When I get into my room, the room is silent. Looking over at the crib, I see Bexley sleeping with her thumb in her mouth. Walking over to her, I run a clean part of my finger gently over her cheek. Walking over to Blade next, I pull his blankets up to his neck and tuck him in the best I can without getting blood on him. Looking over at the bed, I see the outline of Trix's body. The blankets are barely covering her hips.

As much as I want to go over to her and feel her body against mine, I don't. Sometimes, I don't know how I got so fuckin' lucky. Starting the shower in my bathroom, I let the water heat up to as hot as I can stand. Stripping down, I toss my bloody clothes into a pile and pull the shower curtain back. Stepping into the water, I watch as the red that seeped through my clothes runs down my body and towards the drain.

I don't know how long I've been standing here when the curtain is pulled back and my beautiful redhead steps under the spray with me. The water is nowhere near as hot as it was when I first got in. I fully expect her to say something, but she doesn't. Instead, she grabs the soap and squeezes some into her hands. Working the lather into her hands, she starts to rub it over my skin.

I watch her with heavy eyes as I think about all the shit that's happened in the last twenty-four hours.

She doesn't care that I have blood on my hands. She still loves me regardless.

She continues to scrub my body with a soapy washcloth until she's covered every inch of me. Once she's done with that, she grabs the shampoo and starts to lather it up in her hand. Standing on her tiptoes, she runs her fingers through my hair. I lower my body down far enough so that she can reach me without struggling. Her hands run through my hair, and scratch at my scalp, before she runs her fingers along the sides of my shaved head.

I can't help the groan that slips from my lips as her fingernails scrape against my scalp. If anything, it's one of my favorite things. She typically does it after sex and *fuck* it gets me hard and ready to go again. When she's done, I rinse my hair and continue to watch her. Her eyes take in my body and the new wounds that I got from being shot. Turning around to rinse my face that I'm sure has blood still on it, I hear her gasp.

Small hands stroke over my shoulder and lower back, careful not to actually touch the stitches. "Elec," she whispers. I turn to face her, and she looks like she's going to cry.

"Don't," I say, pressing my finger against her lips. She looks up at me, hair soaked through. She's a fuckin' sight. Wrapping an arm around her waist, I pull her body into mine. "I would do it again and again." She nods her head and presses her face into my chest. Water cascades over us as we stand just like this until the water finally goes cold.

Shutting the water off, I open the curtain and grab the towel off the hook. I dry her off slowly, taking my time and memorizing every inch of her skin. Losing her to that fucker isn't an option, and I'll be damned if I let her out of my sight now that I know there is still a threat after her.

Once she's dried off, I quickly dry myself off. Once I toss the towel on the small counter, she grabs my hand and leads me to the bed. I pull the blanket up and she scoots under the covers. Sliding in behind her, I wrap my arm around her and pull her body into mine, holding her tightly against me. I can feel my heartbeat pounding in my ears and I wonder if she can feel it, too.

After a few minutes of silence, she turns in my

arms and wraps her arms around my neck, burying her face into the crook of my neck and the pillow. Her breath fans over my skin as I run my hand gently up and down her back.

"I was so scared that I was going to lose you both," she whispers. Her heart starts to pound, and I can feel every breath she takes. "I can't do this without you, Elec. You might be a bastard ninety-nine percent of the time, but you're mine. You belong to me and the kids." I close my eyes as I listen to her words. "Without you, I don't know what I would do. I tried to live without you and all that led to was a broken heart and more drama than I ever intended. He's a great man, but he's not you. No one is." Her voice breaks, and I feel her tears fall onto my skin.

Grabbing a handful of her hair, I pull her head back so she looks at me. "I know I haven't done a lot to make you trust me, but I will give my life for you and our kids. No question about it." I lower my mouth to hers and take it in a deep kiss. Her fingers grip the back of my neck, and she tries to pull me closer to her. Skin on skin, nothing between us.

She breaks our kiss and my hands travel down her back, gripping her ass cheeks. "You had her blood on you." It's not a question, so I don't give her an answer. She already knows whose blood it was. "I know you did it because of what happened." Her lip trembles and she closes her eyes. "We won't end up like Harlyn and Stavros, right?" Her leg wraps around my hip and her warm, wet cunt is pressed against my dick.

Do I think that we will end up like Stavros and Harlyn? Fuck, I don't know. Part of me thinks we will, but I don't want to say those words to her. They will feed into her fear of us and I don't want that to fuckin' happen. I want us to be a family.

"I won't let us end up like them. I ain't letting you go. You're mine, baby girl, and there is nothing that will change that." A small smile forms across her lips and I press my mouth to hers. "Never losing you again," I murmur before I slip my tongue into her mouth and kiss her like I'm a starved man. Fuck, if I'm being honest, I am. She pushes me, so I have to roll over onto my back.

She straddles my waist, leaning to kiss her way down my neck. She sucks on one of my nipples and rubs her sweet cunt against my length. I harden even more with her slow strokes. When I can't take the teasing anymore, I grab her hip and stop her. Holding her in place, I reach down and grab my dick, stroking it a few times before I rub it along her slit. Her tits bounce as I move her up and down.

When I slowly slide her down on my dick, her eyes widen and her fingers dig into my chest, no doubt leaving marks on my skin. She grinds down on me and starts to rock her hips. Every move of her hips brings me closer to the edge, and I know it's not going to take me long to come. It's been a shitty day, and my body is fuckin' amped up already. My hands roam her skin, caressing and squeezing as I go.

She starts to ride me faster, chasing her own orgasm. I can feel her cunt tighten around me, and I reach up to grab her hair. One thing that gets her even hotter is when I pull her hair as I fuck her. Wrapping her hair around my fist, I pull her head back. I can feel her pussy pulse on me as she slows her movement. Her back is bowed and her eyes are closed. Her mouth parts, and I can see the quiet whimpers of pleasure written all over her face.

I thrust my hips up and into her hard. Every thrust is deliberate and I'm chasing both of our orgasms. "I'm going to come," she breathes. I sit up enough to bring my mouth to her nipple and continue to fuck her hard. The bed hits the wall, and I can't even focus on keeping quiet anymore. The only thing I can think of is coming and falling over the edge with my girl right there with me. Her hands go to my head and she scratches my scalp with her nails, triggering me to come instantly. I watch her as she bites her lip, trying to muffle the sound of her crying out my name in ecstasy. "Elec," she whimpers.

I release her hair and she sits up on me, slowly sliding up and down me. I claim her mouth roughly, and swallow the sound of her whimpers and ragged breathing. "I love you, E."

Kissing my way down the side of her neck, I murmur against her heated skin. "I love you, too, babe." She sighs in contentment and lowers her upper body onto mine, burying her face into my neck.

We lay like this for a while before my phone starts vibrating. She groans when she moves off of me and grabs it off the side table. When she hands it to me, I see Ro's name on the screen. "Yeah?" I answer softly.

"Church." He doesn't say more than that and, with a click, the line goes dead. Looking at Trix's face, I can see the love she has for me shining through. If I didn't have her by my side right now, I don't think I'd make it through this shit. The lies and betrayal are too fuckin' much. She doesn't know that she's saved me on more than one occasion.

Sighing, I kiss the top of her head and roll her over to her back. "I'll be back."

"You're not leaving, are you?"

"Naw, we have church. There's a threat on you. Have to figure out the plan. I'm going to have a prospect outside the door until I get back." Her body stiffens and her eyes search me.

"Why is someone after me?" she asks, sounding frightened.

"I killed his brother when I was eighteen. Now,

he wants revenge." Her gasp fills the room, and I look over to the kids to make sure they are both still sleeping. "Everything is going to be fine. I won't let anything happen to you. You've been through enough the last year." Her arms wrap around my neck, and she pulls me down for another kiss. She kisses me almost like it's going to be the last time.

"I love you, baby. You are my angel." I run my fingers softly down her cheek.

"Love you, Elec," she whispers, closing her eyes. I lean down and kiss her once more before getting out of bed and getting dressed.

Shooting a text off to Romeo, I tell him to have a prospect outside my door in case someone else gets into the clubhouse while we are in church. By the time I'm dressed and about to walk out the door, I see the look on her face. Although she doesn't like the shit I do for the club, she understands that it's part of the territory.

Trix has never made me out to be something I'm not, and I am sure to let her see all aspects of me. She's seen the anger, the rage, the hurt, and the happiness.

Even through everything she still loves me.

Walking out the door, I shut it softly and see one of the prospects coming towards me. "Don't let anyone in or out of this room." He nods his head and stands in front of the door without a sound.

Making my way towards church, I watch as the rest of the men start to make their way inside. It's a little after five a.m., and most of these fuckers aren't morning people. I take my seat and wait for the doors to close.

When Prez takes his seat, the doors shut and the gavel is slammed down on the table. "Thanks for comin' in early boys. You know I wouldn't be pullin' your asses out of bed without a good reason at this time." He looks around the room at us before he continues. "As most of you know, Easy E has been nomad for the last year and a half. I'm bringing him back into the fold as a patched member now that his shit with Ro is done. No bitching or grumbling against it. I've already made my decision." The room stays silent. No one will go against his ruling.

I didn't even know he was going to bring me

back. I sure as hell didn't ask him to. I made my decision almost two years, and I was fine with staying nomad.

"I also invited Tarak to sit in with us this morning because he's got some helpful information about what we are about to go up against. I'll let E fill you in on what happened after we brought back his daughter." Prez nods to me and I sit up a little straighter. All eyes focus on me and my mind crashes through the images of Mica and the blood that sprayed all over me as Romeo slit her throat.

My eyes shoot over to Tarak, and he's looking down at his hands. "We spoke with Mica earlier, and she finally gave up the identity of the other person behind the attacks on me and Trix. His name is Allen Gloscal. I killed his brother Sam when I was eighteen. The charges were dropped because I claimed self-defense, and Tarak testified at the trial in my defense by saying he came after me and I stabbed him because of it." When no one says anything, I continue.

"Mica was convinced to help Allen get revenge on me by getting Trix out of the picture. I guess Mica has had some crush or something on me, and it didn't take much to convince her to do it. She killed Tina and tried to frame Trix for her murder, which I took the fall for." I look over at Tarak and, this time, he's watching me.

"Mica mentioned that she hoped he kills Trix. I'm assuming that she is the target of his plan, but I'm not ruling out my kids either. They are going on lockdown until we can deal with this shit." My hands grip the chair as I think about that bastard. I don't know what his plan is, but I won't let him follow through with it.

"Tarak, what do you know about this fucker?" Prez says from the head of the table.

He clears his throat, and looks down at his hands, before he speaks. "My senior year, I started dealing for him. I got hooked and snorted more than I was selling. When Sam found out about it, he threatened to tell his brother and I knew that it would lead to me being killed. I tried to hide my habit from E, but he figured it out and promised he'd help. E dragged me to an abandoned warehouse one night, swearing that he'd set Sam straight and was going to help me get clean."

I watch as he picks at something on his jeans. "When Sam showed up, he was pissed that we were stealing from him and was going to make an example of me. He reached for something, but E stabbed him before he come at me." He stops talking and turns his focus on the ground.

The room is silent for what seems like forever. " A few months after I got clean, Allen found me. He said he knew about what we did and that he'd make us pay. I sat on pins and needles for the next year, but nothing ever happened, so I let it go. I thought that maybe he let it go too, but apparently not."

Everyone's attention turns back to Prez. "Retribution is what this asshole is looking for, and we aren't letting him take one of our own for that. We will protect what's ours." Heads around the table nod and Mirror looks at me.

"You sure he's coming after your ol' lady? If I were him, I'd go after your legacy." I look at Prez and he nods in agreement.

"Hit you where it hurts," Prez says, before looking back over at Tarak. "What do you know about where they hang out?"

"Last I heard, a warehouse just outside of town on Millsaw Road."

"I want a fast and hard strike. I want us to take their whole damn operation out. Let's make a goddamn statement not to fuck with us. He'll regret ever coming after one of ours."

Chapter Twenty-Five

Once a majority of the plans were made, Prez released us and told us to rest up. He wants us to strike before they have time to strengthen their defenses. Me, I just want this shit over. I don't want my girl to constantly be looking over her shoulder, wondering when someone is going to strike. I don't want my shitty decisions to come back on my kids either.

We all watched Stavros pay for the sins he committed when he took the place of Trix. When he came back, he wasn't the same man as when he left. He was almost dead when we finally found them. I won't put my beautiful Trixibella through that. The pain of watching someone she loves almost die. No fuckin' way. I want to end this shit before it gets that far.

Allen has been holding a grudge for far too long, and it's about time to end that shit. When I get back to my room, the prospect is still in the place I left him.

"No one came near the door. Your ol' lady tried to come out to get some food for the kids, but I sent Mikey to go get them what they wanted. He should be back any minute." I nod my head and dismiss him.

"Thanks," I reply, opening the door to my room.

Walking inside, giggles fill my ears and I see Blade come running at me. "Daddy!" he squeals, wrapping his arms around me.

"Hey, kid." I lift him up, and he wraps his arms around my neck, squeezing me tightly enough to choke the shit out of me. Walking over to where Trix is changing Bex's diaper, I press a kiss to the side of her neck before going over to the bed to have a seat. As soon as my ass hits the mattress, Blade is trying to do some WWE move that knocks me over.

"Who's been teaching you wrestling moves?" I ask, tickling his sides. He bursts out into a fit a giggles before I'm able to get up on my knees. Leaning down, I tickle him more and he starts to scream and kick his legs in excitement. And here I was hoping to get a damn nap in.

"Unck Tavlos," he squeaks. Of course that's whose been teaching him that shit.

We wrestle for a good ten minutes before there is a knock on the door. When I go to get up, Trix stops me and tells me to keep wrestling with Blade. She sets Bex on the bed behind me before walking towards the door. I watch from the bed as she opens the door and I see the prospect's face poking in.

He's been hanging around for the last year. He's a little older than me, but we've never had a problem with him. He seems like a good guy. He keeps his head down most of the time, and cleans up our messes without a complaint. His eyes meet mine, and I see something flash in them. Bex grabs my shirt, and tries to pull herself up, just as I hear Trix yell something, and then I hear it.

Bang.

Both kids freeze, and Blade grabs his sister, as I jump up from the bed and take off towards where Trix is falling to the ground. The gun is pointed at me now and I run full force right into him, knocking us both out into the hall before he can pull the trigger again.

I don't hear the screams as they fill the air. The only thing I'm thinking of it the bastard I'm straddling, letting my fists fly into him without regard of what I'm doing to him. I keep hitting him, blood pooling all around us. Arms wrap around me, and I'm being pulled back. I fight with whoever has a hold of me. The blind rage I'm in keeps me fighting, not caring who the fuck it is that's trying to stop me.

"Elec." My heart stops for a second when I hear her voice floating in from the haze around me. The darkness I was just in starts to evaporate and, soon, I stop fighting. "Please, Elec, stop." Her voice breaks and, when I focus on her, I see the blood seeping through her shirt. I pull out of someone's grip and run to her. I fall to my knees next to her and Stavros. My hands go to her body and she winces.

She's still on the ground and, when I look over her shoulder into the room, I see the scared expressions on the kids' faces. "Stavros," I whisper. He looks over Trix's shoulder and sees the expressions on their faces, too. He gets up and tells Ro to stay with us until the doc shows up. He makes his way to my kids and shuts the door behind him.

They don't need to see this shit and they don't need to know the type of man I am deep down. I won't ruin them. I can't ruin them. They are too pure to be consumed by something so dark. I hear Blade screaming for me through the closed door. Looking back down at Trix, I focus my attention on her. "Where are you hit?" I ask.

Her hand slowly moves down to her side and tears fill her eyes. "He was going to shoot…" she trails off. A tear slips from the corner of her eye, and I hear more commotion going on in the bar area.

"Let the doc through, assholes," someone yells from out there. I see the top of her head as she pushes past the men watching the scene in front of them. When she reaches us, she kneels down and starts to pull Trix's shirt up to examine her.

Trix's hand is in mine as I watch the doc poke and prod her. She winces every time the doc puts too much pressure near the wound. Instead of watching,

Romeo looks over at the guy on the floor a few feet to our left. He reaches out and feels for a pulse. When his eyes meet mine, he shakes his head no. Standing up, he makes his way towards the other brothers.

That motherfucker is lucky he's not alive still. I would slowly torture the fucker for shooting my girl, if he was.

The room starts to clear and Trix's hand gets clammy. She's having trouble breathing as the doc pulls the bullet from her side. "E, I need you to grab this vein right here. She's losing a lot of blood and I can't stop it on my own." I release Trix's hand and do exactly as the doc says. I hold some tweezers in my hand while she continues to dig into of Trix's side.

"Elec," Trix whimpers. My eyes meet hers, and she looks almost like she's about to pass out.

"No, I need you to stay with me, babe," I demand. She tries to nod her head, but it barely moves.

"Just protect them," she says on a harsh breath. No, there is no way she's leaving me. No fuckin' way. Not after everything we've been through.

"Trix, baby, I need you to keep your eyes open.

You aren't going anywhere. We just finally figured this shit out. I'm not losing you yet." Anger is starting to fill my veins and, when I look up, I see Tarak standing close by. My eyes meet his and he looks regretful. He thinks this is because of him, which yeah I blame him for part of it, but not all of it. He brought that bastard into our lives, but I was the one who killed his brother.

He wanted redemption, looks like he just might get it. "Here, hold this with your other hand. I need to get as much blood out of the wound as I can." The doc hands me something that looks like a branding iron before taking gauze and stuffing it into Trix's wound.

"Ahh." Trix screams out in pain as the doc puts pressure on her wound. Her eyes roll back in her, and her body goes limp against the floor.

"Trix!" I yell. I'm frantic, but I never release the things the doc wanted me to hold. Doc reaches across and puts two fingers to her throat, waiting a few minutes before she nods her head.

"The pain is probably what caused her to pass out. She's still breathing, and her pulse is getting a little stronger." The doc continues to work on her, and I just watch as the love of my life lies on the ground in a puddle of her own blood.

She took that bullet to protect one of us. It could have been me, Bex or even Blade who took that bullet if she didn't get in front of it.

By the time the doc gets the bullet out, and her stitched up, it's been three hours. The blood that I was soaked in is now dried. My hand keeps going to Trix's throat to make sure she's still breathing. "E, I want to move her somewhere more comfortable. Do you guys have an extra room that's clean?" I look up at Romeo and he nods his head, motioning to us to follow him.

Picking Trix off the ground gingerly, I follow him with the doc right on my heels. She's got an IV of something in the air as she keeps stride with us. Ro opens the door to Stavros's room and I walk her over to the bed and gently set her on the bed. "Stavros wants you guys to use the room as long as you need. He's got the kids." I nod my head and, when I go to say thanks, a lump in my throat keeps me from saying anything.

He nods his head in understanding and closes the door behind him. The doc hangs the bag above the bed on some nail that was holding a photo up. She sets the photo on the table next to the bed and when I look at it, I see Harlyn and Stavros smiling. It is a few years old, but I know why he keeps it. He doesn't want to let their memory fade. I'd be the same damn way if it were me in his position.

The doc pats me on the shoulder before telling me that she's going to head out. "I'll stop by to check on her in a few hours, but I have rounds I need to make at the hospital." I nod and watch her walk out of the room.

A knock a few minutes later doesn't even get a response from me. The only thing I can do right now is watch her chest as it rises and falls with each labored breath she takes. The door opens, and I see Romeo stick his head in the room. "Brought you guys some clothes. I'm sure you want to get out of the bloody ones." I nod, and he sets them on the bed. His eyes travel over her body before he swallows audibly. "You holding up?" he asks, not taking his eyes off her.

"Yeah. Thank you for everything." I have to clear my throat as soon as the words leave my mouth.

"You really do love her," he states, almost like he never believed me when I said it before.

"Yeah. I have for what seems like the whole damn time I've known her." He doesn't say anything more than that. He takes one last look at her before he turns and walks back out the door.

I spend another twenty minutes watching her before I get up to shower. Once I wash my body, and scrub the lingering blood off my skin, I shut the water off and dry off. Once I'm dressed in a pair of sweats and a plain white tee shirt, I grab a rag and wet it with warm water. I need to get the dried blood off her too.

Walking to the bed, I take a seat next to her body and pull her shirt up enough so I can clean the blood off her skin. I slowly take my time, making sure that she is free of any blood before I change her into a tee shirt of mine. Leaning back against the wall next to her, I watch her. An hour later, I hear a slight knock before the door cracks open. "You guys decent?" Stavros asks.

I chuckle to myself and tell him yeah. I watch Blade come into the room hesitantly. His eyes land on his mom before they turn to me. Tears well up in his eyes, and he starts to rub his nose that looks just like his momma's. I wave him over and he comes willingly. I help him on the bed, and he takes a seat next to me. His eyes never leave his mom. "Is Momma okay?" he whispers.

Stavros brings Bexley to me, so I take her from him and pull her against my chest. Her small arms wrap around me and, for the first time since that door opened and the shot was fired, I feel like I can breathe. I was so damn scared of losing everything. In the blink of an eye, I almost did. Losing Trix would ruin me.

"Sorry, man, they wanted you."

Looking over at him, I nod my head in understanding. "Don't worry about it. I'm glad they are in here with me now." I swallow the lump in my throat before I say anything else. "How did you do it?"

He shuts the door, shutting the outside noise out. "Come back from almost dying, or losing the love of my life?" I watch him take a seat on the chair across the room from me.

"Both, I guess," I shrug.

"Losing her the first time was harder than this

time. She's been halfway out the door since I dragged her ass back. I knew better than to assume she wouldn't run again with the shit we went through. My only advice is to love her through it. When she wakes up, don't give her the option to walk away." He sighs and runs a hand through his hair before continuing. "Most of all, do it for them." He motions to the kids who both have their eyes on Trix's still body.

"You'll struggle, hell we all do, but never give up on each other." I nod my head and look back over to my Trixibella. I can't imagine my life without her in it. I don't want to either. She and the kids are what matter most to me now. The club with always be a love of mine, but my family will always come first.

"Did we find out who he really was?" Stavros grimaces at my question, and I know the answer already. "It was him?" He nods, not saying the words out loud.

"Not sure why he went full on suicide attack on her. Maybe he didn't care how it ended, as long as he took someone in your family down with him. An eye for an eye kind of thing." Bex curls herself into my body, and I run my hands down her back, trying to soothe her antsy ass. She wiggles around more than Blade ever did at her age.

"Thank you."

"No thanks needed, brother. It's what we do." I nod my head and he stands up to leave. "Use the room as long as you need. I'm going to set some stuff in motion to finish this shit. He may have been able to fake his way in here, but I'm not letting *any* of his people survive this shit. Stay with your kids, and make sure she's okay when she wakes up. The doc will be back in a few hours."

Chapter Twenty-Six

Eight Hours. Twenty-Six Minutes.

That is how long it's been since she went unconscious. The doc swore up and down that her body is healing itself and that's the reason for her to still be unconscious. My patience is wearing thin. I want to see her beautiful fuckin' eyes looking back at me already. I want her to tell me that everything is going to be fine. That we are going to make it pass this shit.

The doc helped me move her into my room, so we weren't taking over Prez's room more than we already did. By the time they got back from the job we planned for Allen's drug ring, I couldn't sit still any longer. They gave me a rundown, and told me that everything went smoothly, but it didn't matter. She was still unconscious with no sign of waking up.

I make myself somewhat busy after a while, making sure to feed the kids, and to give them both a bath. By the time I've gotten them into their jammies, and cuddled up on the bed with Trix, I'm ready for a drink.

Walking over the drawer beside the bed, I open it and see the box I left in there. When she left, I never wanted to see it again. Grabbing it out of the drawer, I open the small black box and stare at the diamond ring.

I bought the ring a while back before everything went to shit. I never intended on asking her to marry me because I was already married, but I wanted her to have it as a promise… a promise that I would never hurt her again. Hell, maybe even ask her if I got divorced.

Now, the only thing I want to do with this ring is put it on her finger and promise her forever. Fuck it. Stavros said not to give her the option to leave when she wakes up if I want her. I'm not letting her get away again. I've done it before, and I was fuckin' miserable. I didn't have her, and I didn't have Blade.

I can't imagine my life without the three of them. Tucking them into bed every night and waking up to their giggles and slapping of feet on the floor. Pulling the ring out of the box, I shut the box and put it back in the drawer, closing it. Sitting on the edge of the bed, I grab her left hand and slip the ring on her ring finger.

My heart constricts at the sight of it on her finger. It looks damn perfect on her hand. Running my hand down the side of her cheek, I lean forward and press my lips against hers. Closing my eyes, I pull away and look over at the kids who are cuddled together in my spot. Not bothering to move them, I get off the bed and make my way over to the chair in the corner of the room so I can watch them all sleep.

I fiddle around on my phone for a few minutes before I just go back to watching them. I don't want to miss any more time with them. Getting up from the chair after an hour, I make my way out of the room and towards the bar.

Everything is dark, and there isn't a sound. I don't remember the last time this place was this quiet.

Maybe the night we brought Prez back, but that was more out of respect than anything else. That day was one of the longest of our lives and there were a few gunshot wounds that proved it.

Walking to the bar, I grab a bottle of Jim and make my way back to my room. Sneaking quietly back into the room, I see a head pop up. When I close the door, I see his shoulders sag almost in relief. He's afraid that something else is going to happen. Setting the bottle by the chair, I take a seat and motion for him to come over to me.

He tucks the blanket around his sister before slowly getting off the bed to come to me. He's wiser than his almost three years. He shouldn't have to live in fear. "Daddy," he whispers loudly. I pick him up to sit in my lap and he cuddles into my chest.

"I got you, buddy." I press a kiss to the top of his head and close my eyes. "I don't want you to be afraid. Your momma and I will always protect you and sissy." I feel his head nod against my chest, but he cuddles to me tighter.

"Who prodect you, daddy?" his small voice

asks.

"Your Uncle Stavros, and the rest of the guys around here." He watches me for a second before he nods his head and lies back against my chest.

"Wuv you, daddy." I kiss the top of his head and just hold him.

"Elec." When I look up, I see her eyes on me. She lifts her left hand up to wipe the tears from her face and she notices her new jewelry. Her eyes widen and then snap back at me. "Is this…" Her voice is a sexy rasp. I watch as she swallows a few times before she tries to speak again.

I get up from the chair with a sleeping little boy. Setting him on the bed, I go to sit in front of Trix. She has tears streaming down her face. Cupping her cheek, I lean down and press my lips to her forehead. "This is my promise to you. I won't live without you or the kids ever again. Almost losing you was torture enough. I watched as you took a bullet to protect us. As pissed as I am that you did it, I get why you did. I'd do the same damn thing for you guys. But don't ever fuckin' do it again. My heart can't take the thought of losing you."

I press my mouth to hers and kiss her softly. Her left hand wraps around my neck and she runs her nails along my scalp like she always does. "We can get married, we can keep doing shit the way we are, or whatever. I don't give a shit as long as I have you."

"I love you, Elec," she whispers against my lips.

"You have no fuckin' clue how much I love you darlin'."

After the longest week of my life cooped up in my damn room at the clubhouse, I finally was able to move Trix and the kids back to the house. Having room to move around is a fuckin' blessing that I never expected to want or need. My ass is currently lying in bed while Trix is putting the kids in their rooms. Last night, she told me that a wedding wasn't something that she needed. I'm not an idiot even if I act like one sometimes, but I could read between the lines.

She wants to get married, but is afraid of it

changing shit between us. To me, it doesn't fuckin' matter. I'll take her any way I get her. When the door opens, I see her red hair tied up into a messy bun and the neck of her shirt falling over her right shoulder. Her bare feet pad across the hardwood flooring, and she crawls on the bed towards me.

"The holy terrors are asleep, and I'm exhausted." She falls onto the bed next to me, and I can't help but grin. She may be tired right now, but I don't care. She's going to be riding my dick in a few minutes. It's been too damn long since I've been inside of my girl. Her stitches came out yesterday, and the only thing I can think of right now is her sweet, warm cunt being wrapped around my dick.

Running a hand down the side of her neck, I watch her for a second. Her eyes meet mine after a few minutes, and she gives me that sly smile that goes straight to my dick. She knows what I want and doesn't hide the fact that she wants it, too. "Elec." Her voice is no higher than a whisper. She crawls towards me and straddles my lap. "What if I said I wanted one more?"

"I'd say I'm game for whatever it is you want. I

love you, and if you want to chase after three of my kids, then more power to you." She smacks my chest, and I reach up to wrap my hand around the back of her neck. Pulling her mouth down on mine, I continue. "In all seriousness, you want another, I'll give you another. Hell, I'll give ten if that's what you want. The only thing I want is you and our family." Her grin lights up the room, and she closes the distance between our mouths and kisses me roughly.

Gripping the bottom of her shirt, I pull it up and over her head. Her tits are on full display, and I can't help but lean forward to pull one of her nipples into my mouth. Her hands grip the back of my head and her nails rake over my scalp. Flipping her to her back, I slide my body between her thighs. Grabbing the tiny ass spandex shorts she's wearing, I slide them off of her and sit up on my knees. Just looking at her body brings every nerve ending in me alive.

Every inch of her skin is goddamn perfect. I can see her stretch marks that she hates, the small belly that she swears she'll never get rid of, and the wide hips that she curses me for. She blames me for these things, but I don't care. They show me exactly everything we've been through. Even the brand new scar that is still pink shows me everything I need to know about her. She loves our kids and me more than anything in this world. I couldn't be fuckin' luckier if I tried.

Kissing my way up her thighs, I slowly make my way to her pussy. As soon as my tongue swipes at her sweet cunt, her hands grip the back of my head. I work her up quickly and her moans fill our bedroom. Sinking a finger into her sweet pussy, I probe her with my tongue in sync with my finger. Looking up at her, I see her head thrown back and her thighs tighten around my head.

My dick is straining against my jeans, and the only thing I can think of now is getting inside of her, filling her up with my cum, and claiming her as mine for the rest of our goddamn lives.

Slipping out of my jeans quickly, I crawl between her thighs and stroke my dick a couple of times. Her eyes land on me, and they slowly make their way down my body before stopping on my dick. "You want this?" I ask, squeezing my dick before I start to stroke it again. She bites her bottom lip and nods her head. "I need the words from you, baby." I run my fingers through the precum that is starting to gather at the tip.

"Fuck me, Elec. I need your dick in me." A smirk forms on her lips, and I can't hold back any longer. She knows the words that get me to fuck her hard and fast. Anytime she tells me that she wants to fuck me, I pretty much fall to my knees and give it to her. She's the only woman who has ever had this type of hold on my dick and me. She completes me in every sense of the damn word.

Running my dick along her wet cunt, I tease her a little before I sink into her sweet heat. Her legs wrap around my back, and I slowly thrust in and out of her. Every thrust is deliberate, and her feet dig into my back, pulling me closer to her body. Leaning down, I claim her mouth and grab her hands, bringing them above her head.

I alternate each thrust to be deep and hard, then slow and tender. Her nails dig into my back and she moans out my name. "Fuck," I grit out when her pussy starts to pulse around me. I feel her body tighten under mine and I pump my hips faster into hers.

"I'm going to… Ahh," she moans. Her cunt squeezes me tightly, and I continue my pace, thrusting into her roughly until I'm coming right behind her. My whole fuckin' body tenses as I spill my cum inside of her.

Collapsing on top of her sexy as fuck spent body, I run my mouth along her neck and collarbone. Her arms wrap around my neck and she sighs. "God, I love you Elec." Her hand runs down the back of my head once more before they fall to the bed.

"I know you do and fuck if I know why half the time. You definitely deserve way more than a man like me." She cocks her head to the side to look at my face.

"I don't know either, but I'm glad you came into my life. You saved me from myself. Before I met you, I was heading down a path that would have been worse for me. Being with you turned me around, and you breathed a life into me that I never knew was possible." I go to say something, but she puts her finger to my lips.

"I love you, Elec, and you and the kids are the best things to ever happen to me. I can't thank you enough for everything you've done for me."

"I haven't done anything. You've done it all, babe," I whisper against her skin. "Thank you for loving me even when you couldn't stand me. I know Ro is probably the better choice for you and the kids, but he will never love you the way I do." She grins at me and pulls my mouth to hers.

"He isn't you. I only want you." I kiss her deeply and my dick stands to attention. A wicked grin appears on her face and she pushes me onto my back. Climbing on top of me, she rides me just like I want her to.

I'm the bastard and she's the angel who loves me.

The End <3

About the Author

K. Renee is from sunny California. Creative by nature, she decided to put her imagination on paper. During the day, she works in an office; at night, she writes. These stories have been in her head for years and are finally coming out on paper.

http://kreneeauthor.net

https://www.facebook.com/kayreneeauthor

k.renee.author@gmail.com

Tsu: KReneeAuthor

Twitter: k_renee_author

https://www.goodreads.com/user/show/36533772-k-renee

Acknowledgements

First and foremost, I want to thank everyone for buying this book! I never thought I would be releasing one book, let alone writing as many as I have in this short amount of time.

I can't wait for everyone to meet my characters and fall in love with them like I have.

I want to thank my beta readers for giving their honest opinion about the book and my in house beta reader (mom)... You ladies are awesome! Thank you for taking time out of your schedules to beta read for me. I am thrilled that you loved these characters as much as I did.

A big thank you to TCB Editing for doing their editing magic for me. I love getting their feedback on scenes. It truly helps!

To my street team, K's Wayward Ladies... Thank you for all you do! You girls are amazing at pimping my book out to the indie world. Thank you for your support and I can't wait to see what the future brings.

To the readers and fans… I thank each and everyone one of you who come to hang out with me during takeovers, participating in my giveaways! I hope you like this and my future books.

-K

Made in the USA
Lexington, KY
23 May 2017